GOAL

ST. LOUIS SIRES: BOOK 1

ALEXANDRIA HOUSE

PROLOGUE

MALEEK

TEN YEARS AGO...

"Man, you crazy! You think Jordan can beat Mamba?! You out your mind!" Jerrell Hunter said as we walked home from school.

"You just saying that 'cause you don't know your ball history. Jordan is the man, a legend! Ain't nobody on the court today that can beat him," I countered.

"Whatever. Just because you be researching stuff don't mean nothing."

"Yeah, it does. It means I know what I'm talking about, and you don't," I quipped.

"Yeah, yeah. So, what you researching now? Some crazy shit like cricket?"

I laughed. "Nah, I studied that a couple months ago. I'm into hockey right now."

"Like, ice hockey? Man, I swear you the weirdest dude I know. You study every sport under the sun and don't play nothing!"

I shrugged. "Tryna find my passion," I said as we stopped at the end of Jerrell's driveway. We both lived on Stephenson Street. My crib was a couple blocks down the way from his.

"Well, I hope your passion makes your black ass some money like mine will. Tech is where it's at, Jones."

"Yeah, I know. Later."

"Later."

I continued my trek home, passing the identically designed, beige brick structures that filled my subdivision. The neighborhood was quiet, and in a lot of ways, boring. Little Rock was a city, but compared to my life back in Memphis, it felt like I was on a different planet. There was good and bad in both places. Yes, it was calm here, but I missed my mom and my friends. Things were chaotic in Memphis, but it was *home*. Living with my dad in Arkansas was cool, though, for the most part anyway.

When I made it home, I unlocked the kitchen door with the key my dad had given me, stepping inside to the usual silence. My dad and stepmom both worked, so it was just me until like 6:00 P.M. I was more than cool with that. I never felt totally comfortable around my stepmom. I mean, she was nice, but not necessarily warm toward me.

I was in my room doing homework when my door swung open. I expected to get yelled at again for closing it, but I didn't. When I looked up, my dad was standing in the doorway staring at me. I couldn't read his expression, but something told me whatever was about to happen wasn't going to be good.

"Maleek...son, I need to talk to you," he said, his deep voice filling my tiny room.

Setting my pencil down on the top of my desk, I turned my body toward him. "Yes, sir?"

He stood there for a few seconds before closing the door and taking a seat on the foot of my bed, a twin that my long, lanky body had nearly outgrown. I wasn't complaining, though. Back at my mom's one-bedroom place in Memphis, I didn't have a bed at all. I slept on the sofa.

My father was silent as he clasped his hands together and stared at the floor. He was a little taller than me and much wider. I looked a lot like him but had my mother's darker skin tone.

"Son, you know I love you, right?"

Initially, I offered him a hesitant nod, but since his eyes were still focused on the floor, I said, "Yes, sir." However, I honestly wasn't sure what parental love was supposed to feel like at that point. Was it having a nice room and nice things in a nice neighborhood but no real connection with your father, or was it having no material possessions but being deeply bonded to an angelic but emotionally unstable mother? I truly didn't know.

"And I hope you know how much I've loved having you live here with me and Randi."

I didn't respond to that statement. I didn't know how to.

"I...I hate things have to be this way, but I'm gonna have to send you back to your mother."

"Send me?" I questioned. Those two words induced visions of him folding me in thirds like a piece of paper and sealing me in an envelope. I wondered how many stamps it would take to mail a sixteen-year-old boy across state lines. I almost smiled at the absurdity of that thought.

"Yes. Well, I won't be able to drive you because of Randi's condition. She's not feeling well enough to travel, and I can't leave her here alone."

"Oh," I said with a frown. "What's wrong with her? She sick?"

Finally lifting his head to look at me, he smiled. "Morning sickness. Me and Randi are gonna have our own baby. That's why I'm sending you to your mom. She can't handle a teenager right now. Randi, I mean."

A part of me wanted to ask him what happened to all the stuff he said when he brought me here. Where were all the promises he made to give me a better life when he visited me at my mom's for the first time in ten years? What happened to, "I talked it over with my wife and we want you to live with us permanently"? And what exactly was there for her to handle? I was almost grown! She didn't have to bathe or dress me. I washed my own clothes, kept my room clean. She cooked, but not just for me. We all ate the food. How was her being pregnant going to change any of that? Conversely, a greater part of me didn't care to know. That part didn't like living here anyway. It also didn't like living in Memphis. All that part of me wanted was to be an adult and far away from all of it, to no longer be a burden to either of the people who made up my DNA.

"Maleek? Son? Did you hear what I just said?" my father's voice broke into my thoughts.

Ungluing my gaze from where it had wandered to the closed door, I admitted, "No, sir. I didn't hear you. I was...thinking."

"Thinking about Memphis?" he asked.

In response, I shrugged.

"Well, I was saying that you can finish out this week of school here and then take the bus back to your mom on Friday evening."

"Ma already knows I'm coming?" I questioned.

He sighed, nodded, and rolled his eyes. "Yeah, Iesha knows. Took me forever to get off the phone with her when I told her. She cussed me up and down, said I disrupted your life for nothing, that I could've left you there if I was only going to keep you for three months."

Well, she wasn't wrong, but I didn't say that. I didn't say anything. I just nodded and fixed my eyes on the floor.

"I really am sorry, son. Maybe you can come back in the summer and visit, spend some time with your new brother or sister. That'd be good, huh?"

"Yeah," I agreed.

That Friday evening, I boarded the bus back to Memphis. That was the last time I spoke to or saw my father.

1

MALEEK

NOW...

I found my passion at the age of sixteen while sitting on that bus, on my way back to my hometown. That change, that transition, triggered an obsession with the last sport I would ever research—hockey. Hockey helped me forget I'd been discarded by a man I barely knew, even though we shared ancestry. It helped me forget that I soon became forgotten by him. It helped me ignore my mom's issues, her mental illness, the people she let take advantage of her no matter how hard I tried to protect her. Every book I read or video I watched kept me off the streets and out of trouble. My fixation with the Memphis RiverKings kept me sane and hopeful. My dedication to my high school hockey team kept me focused on the future. My desire to be the best lineman in the history of the game caused me to practice my skills to the point where I damn near slept on the ice, and while I was good, it was my intellect that earned me a full ride to an NCAA college. My performance on the ice, however, was what made it possible for me to sign on as a free agent after I earned my degree. I'd been property of the NHL for three years before the Sires were established, and now, I was proud to be a part of this two-year-old team, the one and only NHL team that could proudly boast of being black owned and black coached, not to mention its roster full of black players. Well, except for Leo Bouchard, AKA Robin Stick, our starting goalie, but he technically wasn't white. I mean, he was white, but he wasn't *white* white.

Out on the ice, all the bullshit disappeared—the bad memories, the sad remnants, the failures, the uncertainties. It all faded away, and there was just me, my stick, and that three-inch disc of vulcanized rubber. The fast pace of the game, the desire to win, the energy of the spectators all served as liquid adrenaline to my veins.

There was nothing like that shit.

Nothing.

I loved everything about the sport that saved me—the sounds, the cold, my brothers in the battle. Shit, I even loved the brutality, the fights, the bumps and bruises. Most of all, I loved going to war, but more than that, winning.

Winning was *everything.*

Rapp, our center, had the puck, handling it like the preeminent pro he was. I kept my eye on him, waiting for a pass. Ford, the right wing to my left wing, was in front of us as the opposing defensemen aided their goalie. We were a fierce line, known to fans as *Southern Comfort* since we were all from the south—Rapp from Louisiana, Ford from Texas, and me from Tennessee, of course—and we played with easy determination. We weren't shit to mess with and we were hard to catch, all of us fast as hell on the ice. In short, we made scoring look easy when it definitely wasn't.

Rapp sent the puck my way, and I took possession of it as I continued to advance toward our opponent's goal. In the blink of an eye, I was there, taking a shot over the goalie's left shoulder and...goal!

In an instant, I was attacked by my fellow linemen who slapped my helmet and yelled in celebration. I smiled as I pumped my gloved fist at the excited fans.

NURI

I shot upright in the bed, another nightmare pulling me from a troubled slumber. When would this end? Would it ever stop? It didn't appear so. It seemed I would forever be stuck in this loop of remembrance, whether conscious or not. As hard as I tried, I couldn't forget, I couldn't erase the frightened faces of the usually bold and sassy third graders I was tasked with teaching. I couldn't shut the sounds of rapid gunfire out of my mind. The terror and raw, primal fear I felt was like muscle memory, surfacing as a result of me hearing something as innocuous as a door slamming or popcorn popping in a microwave. Anything, *everything,* was a trigger. Sometimes, nothing was a trigger, nothing at all.

No one died that day at Rogers Elementary School. No one was even injured, but that didn't soothe my pain or extinguish my fears. It was the "what ifs" and "could've beens" that haunted me; the possible *next times* were what made me quit my job. I couldn't quiet the thoughts of a possible second occurrence, the likelihood of another disgruntled man choosing my place of employment to exorcise his frustrations in the form of a mass shooting. So, there I was, lying in bed in an apartment I could no longer afford, just like the therapy I could no longer afford since I lost my insurance when I discarded what was once my dream job. I loved kids and I loved teaching, but there was no way I could stomach the thought of witnessing a student being hurt.

No way.

As I knew it would be a while before I managed to find sleep again, I grabbed my phone to peruse *Indeed* and other similar sites, hoping to find a job that wouldn't induce a panic attack.

2

MALEEK

"You don't like it?" Tasha asked, her deep-set eyes focused on me.

I gave her the best smile I could summon as we stood in the kitchen of the huge, empty house, a newly built, five-bedroom structure that screamed, "I got money!"

"I do," I assured her, "but you know this ain't my thing. I don't know shit about houses. If you like it, I like it."

She squealed, jumping into my arms and raining kisses all over my face. She was so damn tiny—not short, but long-legged and slim, had been since we started dating back in college, almost seven years earlier.

"Yay!" she gushed, stepping out of my arms. "So, you'll get with the realtor and handle everything? I can't wait for us to move in. Decorating this place will give me something to do while you're working…"

I smiled, observing her as she prattled on. Tasha was my ride or die, sticking with me through the good and the bad. Did she have her flaws? Sure, but didn't we all? I cared about her and was honestly thankful to have her. Being a professional athlete was demanding as hell. *Me* being a professional athlete would be hard on any woman because of my obsession with and love for the sport. For me, hockey was my main lady. Any other woman was my mistress. Tasha understood that, and it didn't seem to faze her at all. She stuck with me despite the fact that I was...me.

"...and there's plenty of space to add other structures to the property, like your own ice rink. That way, maybe you could spend more time here with me," Tasha finished, hugging me again. I fought not to stiffen in reaction to the thought of spending more time with her. I mean, I loved her...didn't I?

Of course, I did.

Yeah, I definitely did, just like I loved this new house.

———

I hated this new house.

I *really* hated it.

It was too big, too stark white, and Tasha was doing too much with the furniture and décor. After seven years of us being together, it was like she didn't know me at all. I didn't like shit like all-white couches or glass dining room tables or gold, ornate mirrors. It felt more like a museum than a home, something to look at but not live in. Why did we need five bedrooms for just the two of us? Why did I even agree to this? Why did I buy this place?

Because that's what you do. You please people. Isn't that why you're still in this relationship? To make her happy?

Now, my thoughts were attacking me on top of everything else.

Shit!

It's the truth and you know it.

I sighed as I sat in the living room watching Tasha hang a massive photo of me and her above the fireplace.

She snatched her head around, looked at me, and frowned.

"What? You don't like the picture?" she asked, her pink-painted lips forming a pout. "I thought one from when we first got together would be nice. You know, it will remind us of where we've been as we move forward. Our kids will see how it all started."

Our...kids?

"Nah, I like it, babe," I lied. I hated how I looked in that picture. I was too skinny and so broke that my hairline was perpetually fucked up back then.

See, I told you it was true. Anything to make her happy, even if it makes you unhappy.

That thought made me sigh again.

In less than a second, the photo was staring down at me from the wall and Tasha had perched herself in my lap, her arms looping my neck.

"What's wrong, Maleek? You've been in a mood ever since we moved in."

"Nothing is wrong. I'm just...tired. Moving at the beginning of the season probably wasn't the best thing to do," I replied, and it was the honest truth. This had all been a lot, too much with everything I had going on. Plus, it all happened so fast. A mere month after first seeing the house, we were living in it, but I'd paid for the place outright, and unfortunately, that had expedited things.

"I know, but isn't this better than us being cramped up in that apartment?"

"Babe, the apartment was two thousand square feet, more than enough room for two people."

"Right, *two* people, but what about the future? There'll be more than two of us in the future, baby."

Before I could respond, she covered my mouth with hers, and in true Tasha Washington fashion, the next thing I knew, we were naked right there on the sofa. Thoughts of our possible future had fled, but I knew they'd be back to plague me again. Hell, I wasn't even sure what I wanted my future to look like or who I wanted to spend it with.

NURI

My late granny, whom my family affectionately referred to as Mother Dear, taught me that life is all about balance—highs and lows, dark and light, good and bad. For me, the good came in the form of a new job. Sure, it was a cashier's position at a grocery store, but it was a *job,* and I'd been in desperate need of one. The bad? I lost my apartment and had been sleeping on my friend Coco's sofa. I was appreciative of her hospitality, but Coco had three cats—Luke, Sky, and Walker, who were very territorial, especially when it came to said sofa. So, I kept being awakened by hissing sounds in the middle of the night. That meant I spent my days in a haze of exhaustion. Walker's ass had even scratched me! So, I was forced to do the one thing I never wanted to do—call my Aunt Yvette.

Sitting in my car, I held my breath as the phone rang in my ear, her "Hello," coming as loud and forceful as usual.

"Hey, Auntie. This is Nuri," I replied.

"I know, sweetie. I've got your number saved. Haven't heard from you in a while..."

"I know. Been busy."

"Mmhmm, Terry said you quit that good job you had. You found another one?"

Rolling my eyes at the thought of what else her messy son might've told her about me, I said, "I did, but I took a pay cut."

"Humph."

I fought the exasperated sigh that was dying to come out of me. "Um, so I can't afford my rent right now, and I was thinking, since Mother Dear's house is just sitting there empty...maybe I can stay there for a little while. I mean, she raised me there. It's my childhood home. I'll take good care of it."

"Now, Nuri, you know I can't let you stay there."

"But it...it's been vacant for years! It needs to be occupied."

"Maybe so, but not by you," she rebutted, and then she hung up.

3

NURI

Things were...bad.

Really bad.

So bad that I was considering contacting my ex to seek refuge, but he was my ex for a reason, and even if he *was* a viable option, he'd expect sex in return for shelter, and well, fuck that. My grandmother always said men needed to earn the pleasure of a woman's body, and Errol hadn't earned the right to touch my pinky toe, let alone my coochie. Therefore, I was still on Coco's couch fighting for my life against her mean-ass cats, since she was my one close friend who still resided in St. Louis. I didn't know anyone else well enough to be living with them, and my locally located family? Never mind.

To top it all off, my job sucked big, sweaty balls. People were assholes, my feet perpetually ached from standing for hours, and with what they were paying me, it would take forever *and* infinity for me to save enough to get even the ratchetest of apartments. My aunt's response to my inquiry had literally broken my heart, although it wasn't unexpected. She'd had something against me from the time I was a kid. Most of all, I missed my grandmother so much. Not just because I knew she would lovingly welcome me into not only her home, but also her arms right now. She'd always been my refuge, my protector, and her love would easily pull me out of the sorrow I was nearly buried in at this point. I needed her wisdom and guidance so badly.

Sighing, I sat in my car perusing job websites on my phone. Without my granny, I would just have to rescue myself.

MALEEK

She was doing it again.

Every so often, Tasha would decide to drop hints about her desire to transition from girlfriend to wife. She never outright discussed it with me. She'd just do shit like print pictures of wedding dresses from the internet and put them places I'd see them, like the bathroom counter or on the refrigerator or on the dashboard of my Grand Cherokee. If she wasn't doing that, she was telling me about one of her friends' engagement rings. Or she'd bring up possible wedding venues during dinner.

It wasn't that I didn't think about marriage myself because I did. I thought about what it would be like, how our relationship would change or if it would change at all. I thought about why marriage was so important to people and why it was the expected next step in serious relationships. I wondered why I wasn't in a hurry to take that next step. Hell, I wasn't even sure if I really believed in marriage. Like, was it really something I wanted or was it on my mind because I knew *she* wanted it? I didn't know, and if I was real with myself, I'd have to admit that I didn't care. I didn't care where this relationship went. I didn't care about much of anything other than the sport that saved me, kept my mind miles away from Little Rock, Arkansas, and my father's rejection. Like I said, hockey was already my wife. So maybe I did believe in marriage after all.

With all of that in mind, I did what seemed to be the right thing. I went to a jeweler and bought her a ring. She'd been with me for so long, put up with my brokenness with few to no complaints, and seemed unbothered by my detachment from everything except my job. So, I guess she'd earned this in my mind. This being the fancy-ass restaurant I took her to.

There we sat in *Prima Bella*, an Italian spot Tasha had been gushing about ever since Ella McClain posted a pic of her and her husband eating here on IG. Tasha's eyes were wide with excitement as we settled at the table.

After taking a sip of water, she turned to me and smiled. "This place is gorgeous, and you look so good, baby."

I returned her smile. I knew she'd be impressed with me wearing a suit. I wasn't a fan of dressing up, especially since the league forced us to do it on game days.

"Thanks. You look beautiful," I replied, and she did. She was mouthwatering in a tight black dress that showcased her fit body. Tasha loved working out, and you could easily tell. My girl was gorgeous.

"Thank you," she chirped.

We ordered our entrees—Pasta Pomodoro for me and Ossobuco for her. As we waited for our food to arrive, I listened to her chatter about any and everything, mostly stuff about Ella McClain because she was kind of obsessed with her. She was a true fan of the model, and I guess I understood why...maybe. I mean, Ella was beautiful, but damn, there was more to life than appearance. Much more.

As the evening wound down, we decided on dessert. Actually, I basically had to beg her to order some since she swore she was too full for it. She was three or four forkfuls into her tiramisu before she found the ring. The look on her face was priceless as her mouth dropped open and her gaze shifted to meet mine.

"Maleek, is that..." Her words were soft, breathless.

Standing from my chair, I dropped onto one knee and asked her, "Will you marry me, Tasha?"

Her "yes" was loud and shrill as she reached down, cupping my face in her hands and kissing me. The other patrons in the restaurant applauded, and ten minutes later, Tasha had cleaned her ring of the dessert and was staring at it on her finger. She was happy, just as she deserved to be.

4

MALEEK

"Rapp! Glad you could make it!" I greeted my teammate at my front door, giving his girl a nod. "Good to see you, Mrs. Rapp," I added.

"Hey, Maleek!" she gushed. "And you need to stick to calling me Indira since your friend here isn't like you. I'm still waiting for him to propose."

"Bae, don't start," he groaned. "Anyway, it's your engagement party, Jones. You know I had to be here to help y'all celebrate Tasha finally locking your ass down," Orlando Rapp quipped. This dude was not only the Sires' center; he'd also become a good friend of mine. His girl and Tasha were pretty close, too.

"Yeah, whatever," I said. "Y'all come on in. Tasha's around here somewhere, Indira."

"Oh, I see her!" Rapp's girl said, kissing her dude before leaving us.

"Aw, shit! *Southern Comfort* is in the muh-fuckin' building!" That was Terrence Ford, my fellow lineman, who'd arrived early and had been doing his level best to drink up all my liquor.

"Damn, you drunk? We in the middle of the season, Ford!" Rapp said. "Wait, Jetta left your ass?"

It was a known fact that Ford couldn't maintain a relationship to save his life.

"Naw! *I* left *her*!" Ford drawled, stumbling deeper into my house.

"Where you going?" I asked Ford.

"To find out where Robin Stick found his date. Did you see her ass? Dude *stay* finding baddies. I need me a new one!" he shouted over his shoulder.

"It's because he got more game than you," I told him.

"Shiiiiiiid!" Ford countered. "I'm one hundred percent Nubian warrior. Ain't no way he got more game than me!"

"Man, your light-bright ass ain't no Nubian warrior," I shot back.

Without turning around, he threw his middle finger up at me.

"Ole red hair having ass," I mumbled.

"She left him, didn't she?" Rapp asked me.

"Jetta? Yep," I confirmed. "This morning."

"Damn. Well, he said himself that he shoulda stuck with his wife. Shit ain't worked out for him since."

"Yeah, and that's because she's got his heart. He loves Krystle. I don't think he realized that until he lost her."

"True. Well, I ain't fucking things up with mine, and you on your way to making shit official with yours. Congrats, man."

"Thanks," I muttered.

"Damn, why you say it like that?"

Frowning, I questioned, "Huh? What you mean?"

"You said thanks like you ain't really all that thankful; what's up, man?" Rapp had dropped his usual silliness, his voice staid.

"I..." Shit, I wasn't sure what to say or how to say it. I'd thought proposing would make me happy because it would make Tasha happy, but in truth, it felt like I was going through the motions. Like I was checking shit off a list:

1. *Get a fine girlfriend.*
2. *Propose.*
3. *Get married.*

Hell, at this point, I felt trapped.

"You love her, so everything will be cool. You probably just nervous," Rapp said.

"Uh...yeah," I hesitantly agreed.

He rested a hand on my shoulder. "You do love her, right?"

I'd opened my mouth to answer him when I heard, "Maleek! Baby, come here!"

Tasha.

Sighing, I informed Rapp, "Gotta go," before heading into my living room where Tasha and virtually all our friends and family were celebrating something I wasn't even sure I wanted to do.

————

"Have y'all decided on a date?" Tasha's mom, Kita, asked before taking another sip of her Pinot Noir.

From her seat in my lap, Tasha chirped, "We're thinking about getting married on Maleek's birthday, May twelfth."

"Ohhh, nice! Maleek, your mother couldn't make it tonight?" Kita asked.

Rubbing my hand down Tasha's thigh, I cleared my throat. "No, she couldn't," was all I offered.

Tasha came from money. Her father was a big-time attorney before he passed away, and her mom's family owned one of the oldest Black hair care companies in the country—*Mama Jaxx's Hair Stuff*—named after the founder, Tasha's great-grandmother Jaxxine. Kita was an uppity, self-professed cougar but not malicious. I think she felt sorry for me more than anything.

Nevertheless, I wasn't about to spread my mom's business. Tasha didn't even know she was institutionalized. Then again, Tasha had never been all that interested in my family, even though she knew my history and had met my mom more than once.

"I see," Kita replied. "Well, I hope she's not ill."

"She's fine," I replied flatly.

"Good."

My phone buzzed in my pant pocket. When I fished it out and checked the screen, I patted Tasha's back and said, "It's my agent. Gotta take this."

Rushing into the foyer, I answered his call with, "What's up, Nate?"

"Jones! Good to hear your voice," Nathan Moore boomed in a southern drawl that nearly matched mine. Moore was from Tennessee, too.

"Yeah, same," I offered.

"Uh...I hate to be contacting you with this kind of news while you're celebrating, but I just got a call...someone reached out to me because my number was the only one they could find that's connected to you. They said they tried to email you but didn't get a reply."

"You know I don't be checking my email."

"Yeah, I do, and you know that shit irks me."

"Yeah...so who wants to reach me so bad that they called you at night?" He sounded kind of subdued. This was bad news. "Damn, did the deal with that energy drink fall through? Fuck."

"No...no, the caller was from Arkansas. Jones, your father passed away."

5

MALEEK

I held the phone, my eyes fixed on the wall in front of me, my mind tangled and confused.

"What?" fell from my mouth, although I'd clearly heard him.

"Your father passed away."

"When? Did they say when? How?"

"Nearly a month ago. Heart attack."

I closed my eyes, opened them, and asked, "A month? Who called you? His wife?"

"No, a lawyer."

"A lawyer? Why? They can tell his wife I don't want my dad's shit."

He sighed. "Uh...his wife is...she passed away a year or so ago. The lawyer is trying to reach you about your siblings. They need a home, and you're their next of kin."

6

NURI

I quit the grocery store job.

I tried not to, but it was just too much. Too many people. Too many hours. Too many sounds. Too little control. I wasn't ready. I wasn't over the shooting at the school.

I was scared.

And broke.

So, I still couldn't afford any much-needed therapy. I was lucky my vehicle was paid off. At least there was that.

I also left Coco's after Luke almost suffocated me by sitting on my nose and mouth while I was asleep.

Evil ass cat.

Hence, I was now residing in a seedy motel whilst continuing my job search. On the upside, I'd lost a few pounds since I was on a diet of air and despair, but I swear, shit was going to have to get better... and soon.

7

MALEEK

I wasn't sure what to do. I didn't know these kids. Hell, I didn't even know there was more than one of them until Nate told me. On the real, I didn't know my father all that well, and what I did know was tied to him dumping my ass when I was sixteen. He was dead, I'd missed his funeral, and I didn't feel sad about it. I didn't feel *anything*. I was just... empty where he was concerned. I turned off any feelings I had about him or my time living with him on that bus ride back home.

"Damn, where are you right now?"

Tasha.

My eyes shot down to where she was kneeling between my thighs, her hand around my dick as I sat naked on the side of our bed.

"What?" I muttered, using my thumb and forefinger to rub my tired eyes. Sleep had been evading me like a motherfucker since the call.

"*Where are you?* I'm down here sucking your dick and you're not even in this room with me," she fussed.

"I'm here. I'm hard, ain't I?" I pointed out.

Rolling her eyes, she said, "I didn't say you were dead, just not...present."

I sighed. "I know. Just got all this shit on my mind."

"What? That call from Nate? You're still thinking about that?" She sounded disgusted.

"Why wouldn't I be?"

Standing, she snatched her shirt from the bed. "Because those kids are not your responsibility!"

"I know, I...I understand being alone and abandoned, though."

She was dressed in her shirt and shorts now as she stood over me. "So, you're actually considering this? You don't know anything about taking care of kids, Maleek! Neither do I!"

"But I thought you wanted kids."

"My own kids! I can't believe this!"

She left the room, and I lay back on the bed, my eyes fixed on the ceiling.

When I felt lost or uncertain about anything in my life, I always found myself here, seeking help from my one constant, unwavering ally. My mom.

Since I became property of the NHL and could afford to, I'd been taking care of her. Wherever I went, she went. When I was traded from the Red Wings to the Sires, I moved her from Detroit into a little apartment here in St. Louis. She was currently temporarily residing at the North Point Lodge, a local luxury mental health facility. None of that sterile, cinder block walled state facility shit for my mom. She didn't deserve that.

She had severe anxiety and major depression, and sometimes, they got the best of her. My mom was good, sweet to a fault, and in some ways, childlike, but she loved me. That, I never doubted. She was here in this place now because of a suicide attempt that scared the shit out of me, but sitting across from her at a picnic table with the sun shining on her pretty face in the warm, early October air, I could see that she was doing better, much better.

"...so, you're torn? You're not sure what to do?" she asked, adjusting the bright yellow shawl on her shoulders, her upturned eyes penetrating mine.

"I am. I mean, I don't hate them. I don't even know them. Plus, they're kids. Ain't their fault our father was who he was. I just don't know what to do."

She tucked her lips between her teeth, casting her gaze into the distance. "Hmmm, I can understand how you feel. I really can. Your father hurt you."

"But?"

"*But* like you said, that's not their fault. You're their next of kin, and since the lawyer is reaching out to you, you're probably their only viable option. Your father didn't have much family when we were together, and what little he had is probably dead and gone now. As for his wife's family...well, you know that situation. They never accepted that marriage."

"Yeah...so, what would you do, Ma?"

She smiled, brightening her beautiful face. "Baby, it doesn't matter what I'd do in this situation. This is your life and your decision to make, Poo."

She was right; plus, I knew what she'd do. My mother never turned down an opportunity to help someone in need, even to her own detriment.

"Put yourself in their shoes," she continued. "What would *you* want you to do in this situation?"

I sighed and nodded. I'd been in their situation, and the outcome had fucked me up. No one deserved to feel like that.

No one.

———

Tasha shifted in her seat, releasing another loud, exasperated sigh, but I was too far up in my own head to address her behavior. I was doing the right thing, and I knew it. Still, that didn't quiet the doubts in my mind, and it didn't make this easy. I was young, twenty-six, and these kids were halfway grown. I didn't know shit about raising kids. Hell, I'd only been taking care of myself for a few years.

"What am I supposed to do when you're working? You're barely home! I can't take care of two kids by myself!" Tasha basically whined.

Closing my eyes, I dragged a hand down my face. "We already discussed this. I'ma hire someone to help."

"You should've hired someone already."

"Tash, come on. You know there wasn't time for all that. I'll get it done."

"Hmph," she huffed, uncrossing and recrossing her legs.

"Tash, I'm not trying to put the responsibility on you. It's on me. It was my decision and I made it. I'ma see it through."

"Mmhmm," she hummed, her attitude on tilt.

I leaned in and kissed her cheek. "Thanks for flying down here with me, baby."

She released another sigh. "Of course, I came here with you. I love you, Maleek."

I smiled, was about to make myself say it back when the door to the little room we occupied inside the Arkansas Department of Child and Family Services eased open, and in walked two kids, both sandy-haired with light-brown skin and uncertainty in their eyes, followed by a thin black woman in a navy-blue pantsuit. We met the woman —Karen Grant—when we first arrived. She was a social worker my dad's lawyer, a Mr. Saunders, put me in touch with. I made contact with her via telephone before we left. She was nice and explained, as the lawyer did, that my father left written and notarized instructions for me to have guardianship over his kids in the case of his death. It was actually part of his will. That shit blew my mind. I thought he'd forgotten about me, and maybe he did until he was forced to face his mortality. Anyway, I'd been granted emergency temporary custody for forty-five days, giving a judge time to review the case. If he or she approved of my father's choice of me as their guardian and there were no objections—including from me—I would become their permanent guardian. All of this was crazy, mind-blowing.

The kids.

There they stood, both resembling our father and me. It was crazy that this was our first time meeting each other.

"Adam, Julia, this is your brother, Maleek, and his fiancée, Tasha. Mr. Jones, this is Julia and Adam Jr.," Ms. Grant said with a smile.

"We know him. We watch his games all the time. Daddy is—was always talking about him," my brother, Adam, shared.

My eyebrows flew up, and that was when I noticed the St. Louis Sires Jersey Adam wore. Number eleven. *My* number.

What the fuck?

Tasha didn't say a word, and when I glanced at her, I found her staring at the kids with her mouth agape. I wasn't sure if she was shocked at the resemblance they bore to me or at the fact that they were obviously biracial. I hadn't bothered to share that fact with her. It was part of a collection of things I'd learned to shut out of my mind, but I'd be lying if I said I never wondered if that was why he dismissed me—because I was black, dark-skinned. Maybe he hated his own blackness. Maybe he saw more value in his white wife and half-white kids than he did me. I'd shut those thoughts down long ago to keep from losing my damn mind.

Vacating my seat, I walked a few steps, coming to a stop in front of my siblings—Julia and Adam—proffering them my right hand. "Uh...it's good to finally meet y'all," I said through the lump in my throat.

8

MALEEK

The kids seemed oddly excited about the trip, were stoked to be in first class, and just during that hour or so flight from Little Rock to St. Louis, I learned a lot about Jules and Junior—their preferred nicknames. Jules was the quiet, shy one. Junior talked almost nonstop about anything and everything, beginning nearly all his statements with, "Did you know?" They both loved hockey, courtesy of our father. We all sat in the same row with Tasha and Jules sitting across the aisle from me and Junior, neither of them uttering a word. Tasha was pissed, blindsided, and obviously frustrated, and I wasn't sure what to do about it.

Both kids seemed impressed with our house and were happy to know they had their own rooms, although they weren't decorated. There really wasn't much in either bedroom besides a bed. We'd have to fix that.

We had pizza for dinner, and afterwards, I helped the kids get ready for bed, digging through their suitcases to find their toiletries and pajamas before showing them how to work the faucets in this fancy-ass house. They were all push-button, and it irritated my complete damn soul. There was a whole panel of controls in the showers.

Ridiculous.

Later, as I lay in bed thinking about the game I had coming up in a few days, Tasha kept her focus on her phone. I'd almost drifted off to sleep when she said, "The ad already has two hits."

Frowning, I opened one eye and asked, "What ad?"

"The one I placed on the *Tammy's List* site during the ride to the airport back in Arkansas."

Opening my other eye, I said, "Let me see."

She handed me her phone, and I silently read the ad: *Seeking full-time nanny for two children, ages seven and ten years old. Will be responsible for cooking meals and ferrying to and from school.*

"Full time?" I queried, handing the phone back to her. "Like, they're going to live here?"

"Hell no! There are enough people living here already. *More* than enough."

"Damn, don't you think you're overreacting? They're just kids. They seem cool, well-behaved, too."

"Those kids are big. I'm not taking care of them, Maleek."

"I'm not asking you to, Tash, and you ain't have to place an ad. I was gonna do it."

"Well, it's done. First interview is at nine in the morning. Second one is thirty minutes after that."

"Damn. Uh, okay. I guess I'll have to call Coach about missing practice. This *is* an emergency, after all."

"Yeah, it is."

I wasn't sure what awakened me the next morning until I opened my eyes and saw two figures standing over me. I sprang upright in bed, confused, eyes unfocused, and drowsiness heavy on my brain.

Before I could get my bearings, a voice said, "We're hungry and we don't know how to work the stuff in your kitchen."

Junior.

That was when I realized the two figures were my siblings. I'd legit forgotten about them, but then again, I hadn't even known them for twenty-four whole hours.

I glanced at Tasha's side of the bed where she lay still, probably pretending to be asleep since I knew she was a light sleeper.

"Damn, what time is it?" I muttered, grabbing my phone.

6:00 AM?

The fuck?

Bro!

"Uh, okay," I said through a yawn. Let me...I'll meet y'all in the kitchen."

Satisfied, they bounced out of the room. Another glance at Tasha, and then I headed to the bathroom to piss and halfway get myself together.

After a search of the kitchen, I ended up ordering McDonald's and having it delivered via the *Quickeats* app, since there wasn't much on hand I thought a kid would like. Tasha and I usually had smoothies for breakfast.

I sat with them as they ate, observing them, their faces and our shared features, their rumpled hair, their innocence, trying to imagine how they felt being in a strange place with an older brother they didn't really know. Afterwards, I showed them around the house. Then they watched Disney Plus in the living room. I was in the kitchen reading over the papers Ms. Grant had given me when Tasha appeared dressed in jeans and a t-shirt, hair and makeup perfect, as usual.

"Good morning. You slept hard, huh?" I greeted her. "Didn't hear the kids come in the room earlier?"

"I was tired. Yesterday was a long day," she said as she gathered fruit and vegetables for her smoothie. "Where are they now?"

"Who?"

"The kids. Who else?" she conveyed tersely.

Holding both my hands up, I said, "Damn, they in the living room watching TV. What's with the attitude, Tash?"

"I'm still tired. First interview is in like thirty minutes. You wearing that?"

I looked down at the gray sweats covering my body. "What's wrong with this?"

She started the blender while giving me this crazy look. So, I sighed, stood from the table, and stepped behind her, wrapping my arms around her and saying, "Hey, turn that off for a minute," directly in her ear.

She did, leaning into me a little.

"I know this is a big adjustment. It's all new to me, too, but I really believe I'm doing the right thing."

"I understand that but is this going to be permanent?" she softly asked.

"I don't know yet."

She sighed. "Go change. I don't want your dick swinging all over the place during the interviews. The applicants are women."

Grinning, I kissed her neck, swatted her ass, and left the kitchen.

"Okay, we'll be in touch," I heard Tasha say as I descended the stairs.

"Who was that?" I questioned, watching her close the front door.

"The first applicant."

Frowning, I stared at her for a minute. "You already did the interview? You didn't wait for me? Damn, I told you I would be right back. I was helping the kids unpack."

"One look at her and I knew she wasn't going to work, so it was a very brief interview."

"Huh? What's wrong with her? She got three heads or something?"

"No, I just didn't like how she looked," she said, walking past me. "I need to pee. Next applicant should be here in twenty minutes."

She'd disappeared from the foyer when I turned to look out the window. The woman was standing next to her car, a confused expression on her face. There was nothing wrong with her appearance. As a matter of fact, she reminded me of Tasha—slim, fit, cute. She wore a black dress, and she looked well put together.

Maybe *that* was the problem.

9

MALEEK

She was short, thick—like super curvy—and pretty, *really* pretty, and something about her voice was comforting, soothing. Her smile? Wow! In a different time and place, and under different circumstances—like me not being in a relationship—I would've been interested in much more than nanny services.

This woman was fine as hell!

The second applicant wore black pants and a pink shirt, her hair in long, thick braids. She didn't wear makeup, like she knew she didn't need it. I couldn't take my eyes off her as bad as I knew I needed to look away, focus on the floor, something!

"Your name is...how do you pronounce your name?" Tasha asked, glancing down at the papers this applicant had given her when she arrived. Of course, she'd taken the lead on the interview.

Of course.

"Nuri, pronounced like jury, as in a jury of your peers. It means light. My full name is Nuri Knox, as you can see on my résumé."

"That's interesting. Well, I'm LaTasha Washington—everyone calls me Tasha—and this is my fiancé, Maleek Jones."

Nuri smiled. "Nice to meet you both. What are your kids' names?"

"Oh, they're not ours. We're just, uh...watching them for now," Tasha said.

"They're my brother and sister—Junior and Jules. I have guardianship over them," I interjected.

Tasha shot me a look and I just frowned at her.

"Oh, wow! That's so wonderful of you to take care of them! How old are they? I can't remember if I saw their ages in the ad," Nuri inquired.

"Junior is ten. Jules is seven," I said.

"Yes. So, according to your résumé, you're a teacher?" Tasha cut in.

Nuri's face lit up, her huge, round eyes shifting from me to Tasha. "Yes! I taught third grade for three years. I loved it!"

"But you want to be a nanny now? Why?" I asked.

Her eyes were on me again, the light in them now muted. "I...I wanted to try something new, different, but still work with kids. Seven-and-ten-year-olds are in my wheelhouse. What school are they attending?"

"Uh, I don't know yet. They've only been here for like a day. Gotta sort all that out," I explained.

"I can help with that. I'm familiar with the local schools, including the private ones. I'm assuming you might be leaning toward private schools?"

I shrugged. "Not sure."

"Oh, okay. Like I said, I can help with that," Nuri offered.

"And you cook, have your own car, right?" Tasha asked.

"Yes," Nuri confirmed.

"The job requires working long hours. We need someone to do everything from cooking them breakfast to tucking them in at bedtime. Can you do that?"

"Yes, I'm flexible. Oh, and my latest background check is there with my résumé."

"Great! Do you have any questions, Nuri?"

"Yes...how much is the pay? I didn't see it listed in the ad."

Now Tasha decided to defer to me, shifting her eyes to meet mine and giving me an expectant look.

Clearing my throat, I said, "Um, one thousand per week." I spit that shit off the top of my head, and from the look in Tasha's eyes, I'd evidently fucked up.

"That sounds good," Nuri said. "When can I expect to hear from you all?"

"Oh, you're hired if you can start now," Tasha blurted with confidence. Now it was *my* turn to look at *her* crazy. Like, what the fuck?

"Really? Sure!" Nuri gushed, and just like that, we had a nanny.

NURI

I thought they were going to be white.

My first thought when I pulled onto the property and laid eyes on the huge, dark brick house, was that these were white people, *rich* white people. My second thought was that I didn't care. As long as these people were halfway hospitable and their kids weren't complete demons, I was going to give it a shot. I was literally prepared to beg for the job. Things were too tight for me not to.

So, I was surprised when a pretty Black woman opened the door but not when she looked me up and down with a tinge of disapproval on her face. Women like her, the beautiful, chosen ones, always looked at me that way, as if I were their worst nightmare. A lot of women would rather lose a leg than be fat. It didn't bother me because my appearance was *my* business. I loved myself, always had. That was why I kept quitting jobs—self preservation. It was also why I was very selective about who I let dip in my honey pot, just like my granny taught me to be. Anyway, I wasn't going to let one of the "mean girls" get under my skin. The guy, her husband or whatever?

He was different, and in my mind, seemed mis-matched with her. I mean, physically, they matched. He was tall and handsome as hell with smooth dark skin and these serious dark eyes. Serious but sad at the same time. His voice was cavernous but not menacing, and he was so damn fine in his jeans and white tee. *Too* damn fine. Yeah, they definitely matched physically, but while the woman oozed entitlement and haughtiness, the guy seemed mellow and down-to-earth.

When she told me I was hired, I really wanted to jump up and hug both of them. Yes, even her, but I kept my cool.

"Let me go get the kids so you can meet them," the guy, Maleek, said, standing to leave the lavish living room. I somehow kept my eyes off his ass as he left.

"Good, we're alone," Tasha, his partner, said, her voice almost a whisper. "Look, I don't expect these kids to be here that long. My fiancé has a big heart, too big if you ask me, but as soon as he realizes this is too much responsibility to be taking on, he's going to send those kids back. I'm only telling you this so you won't get your hopes up thinking this is a permanent position."

I'd opened my mouth to respond when Maleek's voice filled the room.

"Nuri, this is Junior, and this is Jules."

I stood, smiling at the two cute kids who, were it not for their lighter skin tone, would be carbon copies of Maleek. "Hi, I'm Nuri," I said, bending a little to look them in the eye. I was short, and at seven and ten, these two nearly matched my height.

"Hi," the little boy, Junior, I surmised, offered. The girl didn't speak.

"It's great to meet you two," I gushed, and it was. They both gave off good energy.

"Are you taking us somewhere else?" Junior asked.

I looked up at Maleek who wore a frown.

"Nah, man...she's gonna help take care of y'all since I have to work and stuff. This is your new home," Maleek explained.

As I stood erect, my eyes involuntarily shifted to Tasha, who looked like she'd just been slapped.

"Okay. We like it here," Junior shared.

"I'm glad you do," Maleek said warmly. "Uh...let's show Nuri your rooms."

And with that, I started my new job.

10

MALEEK

Out of nowhere, the weight of what was going on in my life crashed down on me, and I started feeling overwhelmed as a motherfucker. That probably had to do with the papers I was reading. It turned out there was a reason Jules didn't do much talking. The state's psychologist believed she was suffering from elective mutism as a result of her being the person who discovered our father's lifeless body nearly a month ago. Junior was now her spokesman as she almost strictly shared her voice with him. Then there was the fact that for some reason, it took a month for the state to contact my dad's lawyer and find out he'd declared me his preferred guardian for the kids, and here I was thinking that nigga had forgotten me. These kids had been in two foster homes in that month. The saddest part was that my dad died exactly one year after their mother's death. Junior and Jules probably needed some damn therapy ASAP.

Like you do, a voice in my head said, a voice I'd been ignoring for years.

Junior also had asthma and a peanut allergy—

"Excuse me."

My head shot up to see Nuri standing in the kitchen doorway, a tentative smile on her lovely face. She really was breathtaking.

"Hey, what's up? The kids good?" I asked. She'd already proven herself to be a godsend, fixing lunch for them, helping them organize their things and making a list of what they needed, keeping them company, cooking dinner, and putting them to bed.

"Yes, I'm...I wanted to let you know that Jules is sleeping in her brother's room. Junior said she doesn't want to be in that big room alone."

"Oh, okay. I can understand that."

She didn't move to leave, and she didn't say anything else, but I could tell she wanted to.

"You wanna have a seat?" I offered. "Got something else you wanna discuss?"

She nodded, taking a seat across from me at the table in what Tasha called the breakfast nook, which was located in the huge-ass kitchen.

"So, the kids have been here a couple days?" she inquired.

Leaning back in my chair, I affirmed, "Something like that."

"Um, have you talked to them, explained what's going on?" she asked with obvious reluctance.

"I mean...I guess not. I ...a lot has happened fast. Been tryna wrap my mind around it all."

"I can imagine, but it's been happening fast for them, too. They're just kids and they're confused. Um...were you guys not close before this?"

I dropped my eyes to the table. "I just met them yesterday, actually."

She took in a quick breath. "Oh."

Lifting my eyes to meet hers, I admitted, "This whole thing is all fucked up, but I'll talk to them."

"Yeah, can I say one more thing?"

"Sure."

"I think right now, the priority needs to be you building a relationship with them. They like you, and I think they feel safe here but not necessarily secure. They need security. I know you have to work but—"

"I'll make time for them."

She smiled. "Good. So...I guess my shift is over. See you tomorrow morning? Sevenish?"

"Yeah, that'll work."

"What are you doing?" I asked, although I could clearly see that Tasha was locking our bedroom door.

"What does it look like I'm doing, Maleek? Don't be obtuse," she tossed back.

"I'm not being obtuse. I'm asking you a question."

"Then ask the question you really want to ask."

"Okay. Why are you locking the door?"

"Because I don't want those kids busting in here on us again. What if we're fucking the next time they decide to come in here?"

"Unlock the door, Tasha."

"Why?"

"Because those kids have been through a lot of shit and I'm their guardian. If they need to come in here in case of an emergency, they can come in here. They don't need a lock blocking them. Anyway, I told them to always knock and wait to be acknowledged from now on."

"No."

"Fine, I'll unlock it."

Before I could move, she held a hand up and flipped the lock on the door. "There. Unlocked. Guess you won't be getting any for a while," she huffed as she headed into the ensuite bathroom.

Truth was, fucking was the last thing on my mind, but I didn't say that.

I lay in bed, my eyes on the ceiling as she completed her usual nightly routine of brushing her teeth and doing her skin care. When she finally climbed in bed with me and cut the lights off, I was halfway asleep.

"Why'd you tell them this was their new home?" she asked, making me pop my eyes open.

"Huh?" was my response because I was too tired to discuss *anything* at that point.

"I said, *why'd you tell those kids this is their home?*"

"Because those kids are my brother and sister, Tash. Why you acting like they're the enemy?"

"Who *is* the enemy, Maleek? Me?"

"No...it's death, I guess. I don't know! Tash...shit, what do you want from me? I'm just tryna do what's right! Fuck! Can't you just have my back?"

"I can't have your back when you keep making decisions that affect my life without talking to me! *I* chose this house and decorated it! *I* picked out every piece of furniture in it and now it's *their* home?!"

"But who paid for all that?" I returned.

The lamp on her side of the bed popped on as she sat up, a murderous look on her face. "What the fuck did you just say to me?!"

I sighed. "Look, let's just go to sleep. I'm tired as hell and I got a long day ahead of me tomorrow. We don't need to be doing all this yelling and shit anyway. The kids might hear us."

She stared at me before finally turning the lamp off, settling into bed, and mumbling, "Fuck you, Maleek."

NURI

Didn't we agree on seven? I thought as I rang the doorbell...again. Then I banged the knocker...*again.* I'd been out there trying to get in for thirty whole minutes.

Finally, the heavy front door eased open to reveal little Julia clad in her pajamas and a loud, screeching sound filling the interior of the house. I had yet to step inside when I heard someone barreling down the winding staircase, and then *he* came into view in nothing but a pair of boxers—which, *damn*—with panic on his face.

"Shit, shit, shit," he muttered as he rushed past the door. A second later, the screeching sound stopped and a phone began to ring.

The door flew completely open, and Maleek said, "Come in," as he answered his phone.

Stepping inside the house, I watched his muscular back as he turned to speak on the phone. "No, no...everything is fine. Yes, false alarm."

I was a bit frazzled but managed to give Julia a smile as she stood there looking more than a little rattled herself.

"Good morning," I whispered to her.

Of course, she didn't answer, but she did grab my hand. I, in turn, squeezed hers.

Next down the stairs was Junior with a worried expression on his face making him look older than his ten years that soon eased into relief when his eyes rested on his sister.

Then came Tasha in a silky, yellow robe. "What the hell is going on?! Why are you down here in your underwear, Maleek?"

Ending his call, Maleek shot Tasha a look before giving his attention to me. "Uh...can you..."

"Hey, guys, let's go find some breakfast," I suggested, taking his cue. As we left the foyer, I could hear him and Tasha arguing in harsh whispers.

MALEEK

The morning was crazy.

After Jules opened the door for Nuri, triggering the security system, me and Tasha had yet another fight. This time, I'm not even sure what it was about. She was pissed, and I got it. Her world had been upended. There were two new people in our lives that neither of us planned for. She wasn't the bad guy. No one was, really. Well, maybe my father was, but since he was dead, there wasn't any use in dwelling on that.

Damn, the man was dead, I found out the same time I discovered I had not one, but two, siblings, and I hadn't been afforded a single second to really process any of this shit.

After our fight, I showered, dressed, grabbed the thick file folder full of Jules' and Junior's paperwork, and headed to Sebayt House, a Black owned and run private school Nate put me on to. Before I left, I'd gotten Nuri's take on the place, and she'd highly recommended it. The best thing about the place was their Afrocentric—rather than Eurocentric—approach to facilitating learning.

After enrolling both kids in their program, I headed to the Sires' late morning practice. That's when the fog that'd been crowding my brain since getting the call the night of my engagement party began to thin out, allowing me to concentrate on the drills, my favorite of which were the shooting drills. This was what the game was all about—goals, scoring under pressure with spectators' voices crowding the arena. This? This sport was definitely my first love, my greatest love affair. Nothing, and I mean *nothing* compared to being out on the ice while wearing over twenty pounds of much needed gear. My job could be brutal with all the crashing and checking, but I wouldn't have it any other way.

In the locker room, I sat on the bench, both sad and glad practice was over. I was tired, but I didn't necessarily want to go home.

"You good, Jones? You were beasting out there today!" Rapp thundered, smacking my shoulder.

"I'm cool, man," I replied, grinning.

He dropped down on the bench beside me. "Everything Gucci at home? I ain't talked to you since you got that call during the party."

"It's...I went and got the kids, my siblings. Tasha is losing her shit over it, and I really can't blame her. I'm messed up about it, too, but I'm tryna maintain."

"Wow, yeah...that's gotta be rough, and shit, you still young and them kids are how old?"

"Seven and ten."

"Damn."

"Yep. Got 'em enrolled in school, hired a nanny—"

"A nanny? She fine?" That was Ford's goofy ass, appearing out of nowhere.

"None-yuh," I replied.

"Aw, shit! She must be *super* fine! You got a woman. Stop being selfish. Invite a nigga over for dinner so I can shoot my shot at Miss Nanny."

"Man, shut your stupid ass up!" I laughed. "How you know it ain't a dude?"

"Cause yo' ass wouldn't have said none-yuh if it was. Plus, you got this look in your eye. It's a woman, and your engaged ass is feeling her."

"Oh, shit! Are you, Jones?" Rapp asked, eyes wide.

"Y'all dumb. Like you said, I'm engaged. Plus, I barely know the nanny."

"Aw, hell," Rapp muttered.

Standing, I grabbed my duffel bag and said, "I'll see you two fools later."

Then I left.

11

NURI

Things went smoothly after the crazy morning we had. I got the kids fed, dressed, and off to school with ease after Maleek called and told me they could start today. It was cool the administrator let them begin the day of enrollment.

Although Maleek told me he'd informed them of Jules' voluntary silence and Junior's allergy, I made sure to reiterate those facts to their teachers. The school was small and very nice, state of the art, a place I'd wanted to work at before. I was glad he'd chosen to put them there.

After I dropped them off, I headed to the store to buy backpacks and school supplies with money Maleek gave me that morning. Next, I took a nap because my sleep had been shitty as of late, did a little apartment hunting, and before I knew it, it was time to pick the kids up.

On the way home from school, Junior talked my ear off about his day while Jules stared out the window. When we made it to the house and approached the door, I literally prayed Maleek would be the one to answer it, and he was, greeting us with a big smile.

"Y'all have a good day at school?" he asked, receiving a shrug from Jules—the same response she'd given me—and an earful from Junior, who very obviously admired his big brother, relationship or not.

When Junior finally came up for air, I asked Maleek, "Do you mind getting them a snack? I need to get their school supplies and stuff out of my car."

"Oh, you already got the stuff? I'll get it. I'll meet y'all in the kitchen."

A panic rose in me, and my words came out in a rush. "No, I'll get it. My car is a mess and—"

"Nope. I got it. Do I need a key, or can you unlock it from here?"

Sighing, I hit the button on my key fob. "There you go."

Maleek smiled again. He was so freaking handsome. "See, that wasn't so hard, was it?"

I returned his smile with a weak one of my own and watched him walk out the door until Jules tugged on my hand. I was in the middle of fixing the kids some sandwiches when Maleek returned with the bags of supplies, setting them on the counter. From the corner of my eye, I saw him approaching me and held my breath, silently begging him not to ask me any questions.

"Hey, uh..." he began but was quickly cut off.

"There you are, Maleek! I need to talk to you."

Saved by Tasha.

"A'ight," he answered, pausing before leaving the kitchen, and I finally blew out the breath I was holding.

MALEEK

Tasha didn't want nothing.

I mean, absolutely nothing, calling me out of the kitchen to ask about some towels she bought like I had enough room in my brain to keep up with shit like that when I obviously didn't. So, I couldn't talk to Nuri when I really needed to. I couldn't talk to her about all the shit I saw in the back of her SUV. She drove a nice but dusty, older model Ford Explorer, maybe a 2016 or 2017, and the inside wasn't really that messy; it was just packed full of shit, like household shit. On the real, it kind of looked like she was living in her truck, or at least in the middle of moving or something. Whichever was the case, she didn't want me to see that stuff. That was clear, and for some reason, it made me feel bad. I didn't want her to think I was the type to judge a person based on them having a junked-up car. The back-seat was clear for the kids, so I was cool. Yeah, I lived in a big-ass house, but I didn't even pick it out. I was happy in our apartment. Of course, she didn't know that because she didn't know *me*. Hell, *I* didn't know *her*. I also didn't know my siblings, and as tired as I was from…everything—practice, a new full-time position as Tasha's debate opponent, traveling to meet and pick up two kids, one of which I didn't even know existed, and the biggest of them all, my absent father's death—I still decided to hang out with her, her being Nuri, and the kids that night. Tasha was pissed about it, so pissed that she left without telling me where she was going. Honestly, I was kind of glad. We needed the time apart however brief I was sure it would be.

I helped divide the school supplies and was impressed that Nuri picked backpacks they both liked—a Spiderman one for Junior and a Barbie one for Jules.

"Dang, how you know they would like these?" I inquired as we watched them write their names on the supplies scattered on the living room floor.

"I asked them," she simply said.

Oh, I thought. That made me really observe her with them. Just two days in, she had built a rapport with them. They seemed very comfortable with Nuri, especially Jules. She still didn't speak beyond an occasional yes or no, but I could see she was relaxed with Nuri. So was I because she had an ease about her, a peaceful energy that made you feel like you'd known her your entire life. It was weird but nice. Just that quickly, I liked her. I also liked that she was around so much. She was some much-needed sunshine, light.

At the end of the night, after the kids were in bed in Junior's room, we both stepped into the hallway, and the easiness we'd shared all evening faded. I could literally feel her energy shift after she closed Junior's door.

"Uh...thanks for helping with everything tonight," she said softly.

"No problem. Tryna spend a little time getting to know them," I replied, mentally adding, *and you, too.* I had to blink that thought away because it felt personal, not professional.

"Right. Good. So...I guess I'll go now. See you guys in the morning. Same time?"

"Yeah. I'll be sure to be up so Jules doesn't feel obligated to answer the door and accidentally trigger the alarm again. Sorry about that."

"Oh, no worries. You already apologized, and I talked to her about it. I don't think she'll open the door again without permission."

"Thanks for that. You got my number, right? So, you can call me if it takes a minute for me to answer the door. But I'ma be up."

"Okay." She wouldn't look at me, her eyes on the floor as she clasped her hands in front of her. "Well, uh...goodnight."

"Wait, Nuri...I want you to know I'm not the kind of guy who judges people or thinks I'm better than others. You ain't got no reason to be embarrassed about having all that stuff in your car. I ain't always lived like this."

Her head popped up, her eyes finally meeting mine, relief in them. "Uh...I appreciate that."

"You moving or something?"

"What? Oh, yes...I am."

"Cool. Let me know if you need some help."

"You don't have to do that. I know you're busy with work and stuff."

"I *want* to. Just let me know when and where to be. I'll make time for it."

She smiled, brightening the whole damn house. She had the prettiest white teeth. "I will. Good night, Maleek."

"Good night, Nuri."

She turned toward the staircase then whirled around to face me again. "Oh! I've been meaning to tell you this. You're gonna need to make a doctor's appointment soon. Did you know Junior only has one inhaler?"

Scratching the side of my head, I nodded. "Yeah, I saw that. I'll get on it, boss."

Her response was to laugh, which made me grin.

I walked her to the front door and watched as she climbed into her truck and drove away. I was still standing there twenty minutes later when my phone buzzed in the pocket of my pants. Checking the screen, I read Tasha's message: *I'm spending the night with my mom. See you in the morning.*

I couldn't remember the last time we'd spent a night apart. Even when I had away games, the team usually flew us back home the same night. The text *should've* bothered me, but it didn't. She might have needed a break from me, but I damn sure needed a break from her. So, I climbed the stairs and prepared myself for a night of peaceful rest.

12

MALEEK

I was in the middle of one hell of a dream. Her mouth was on me, pleasing the shit out of me as she sucked and stroked and hummed on my dick while I lay in the bed, my hands tangled in her braids.

"Baby," I muttered. "Don't stop. Shit, don't stop."

"Hmmmm," she responded, but her voice didn't sound quite right. It didn't sound like...her. I was five seconds from calling her name when she stopped sucking, making my eyes pop open. That was when I realized it wasn't a dream, while at the same time, it was. Tasha was home. It was *her* mouth on me, and now her face was hovering over mine as she straddled me.

"Tash? You're here?" I croaked.

She smiled. "Yeah, who else would be sucking your dick?"

"I meant...weren't you at your mom's?"

"I was, but I missed you."

"Oh."

Her brows knitted together. "Oh? That's all you have to say?"

"No, I mean...I thought I was dreaming."

"About me?"

"Yeah," I lied.

Grinning, she leaned in and kissed me before completely freeing my dick from my boxers and sliding down on it. Closing my eyes, I saw her face again, *Nuri's* face—big, round eyes, gorgeous smile. I mentally scanned her entire body, moaning as Tasha rode me. Wait, was it Tasha or Nuri? I opened my eyes and tried to hide my disappointment with a smile as Tasha began kissing me again. What the fuck was wrong with me? I didn't even really know Nuri...but I obviously wanted to.

I barely slept after Tasha ambushed me at one in the morning. Don't get me wrong, the sex was good. It always was because truth be told, Tasha was more experienced than me. When we first got together back in college, I was a nineteen-year-old hockey nerd of a virgin and Tasha was already a veteran at fucking. She turned my ass out in the beginning and quickly won my devotion. Now I was twenty-six, and she was still the only woman I'd ever been with. She was also the only woman I'd ever *wanted* to be with...until Nuri, a woman I met two seconds ago. Like, what the fuck? What the fuckity fuck? Hell, what the fuckity *fuck* fuck?

Yeah, things had been tense between me and Tasha since we picked the kids up, but we were solid. We loved each other. I mean, Tasha definitely loved me, and what I lacked in the love department, I made up for in loyalty. I'd never betray her. I cared too much about her. We had seven years of history, after all, but there was just something about Nuri that was pulling on me, and I had no idea what it was. It didn't help that she was finer than a whole bushel of motherfuckers.

Damn!

To try and shake whatever had me dreaming of fucking Nuri Knox out of my head, I climbed out of bed early, telling a drowsy Tasha that I was going to run out and get breakfast and for her to keep her ears open in case the kids needed something. She surprisingly agreed, and minutes later, I was in my Jeep, headed to Tasha's favorite breakfast spot across town at the ass crack of dawn. It was so early that the streets were relatively clear, so the ride was pleasant. After grabbing a fried chicken biscuit from the little café Tasha loved, I headed down the street to McDonald's to grab something for the kids. The McDonald's was next to a hotel, and I noticed something while in the drive thru line that made me question my sanity. There was a vehicle on the lot that looked like Nuri's, dust and all. Nah, I was tripping, but what if I wasn't? What if it was her truck and she was in that hotel fucking some dude or woman? What if Nuri was a lesbian? I wasn't sure which possibility hurt worse or why the hell I cared.

I really needed to get myself together.

I stared at that car for so long that the person in line behind me had to blow their horn to get my dumb ass to move. I needed to stop this shit. I was engaged and in love and stuff. Plus, I had too much other crap going on to be crushing on some woman who was in my employ.

NURI

I slept like shit...*again*. Something was going to have to give, because at this rate, I was going to have a sleep deprivation stroke or something. At least I wasn't having nightmares anymore as they required actual slumber to occur. Also, I didn't feel as anxious and on-guard working this new job. Another plus? I would get paid in a couple days. We'd agreed on paydays being Fridays. That would fix my issue for sure.

"Hey, thanks for taking care of breakfast. You didn't have to do that since it's part of my job," I said as Maleek led me through the foyer to the breakfast nook.

"It's all good. I was up early this morning anyway. I even got you something," he replied.

"Really? Thanks! You know what? I'll go get the kids up and bring them down."

"A'ight. Thanks."

A minute or so later, I was gently knocking on Junior's door, opening it to find him sitting up in the queen-sized bed rubbing his eyes.

Before I could ask, he informed me, "Jules is in the bathroom."

"I see. Good morning, Junior."

"Good morning, Miss Nuri."

I smiled. "Miss Nuri?"

"Yeah, Jules said we should call you that because you're sort of like a teacher."

"I guess she's right."

Jules emerged from the bathroom, giving me a bright smile and a barely audible, "Good morning."

"Good morning, Jules. You two ready for breakfast?"

Two adorable heads nodded, and we were quickly making our way down the stairs. Tasha was in the kitchen when we arrived, sitting on a stool at the island while eating something that smelled heavenly.

As I got the kids settled at the table, I heard her say, "And you got me two?! Thanks, baby! I'll eat the other one tomorrow."

"Uh, I actually got the other one for Nuri," Maleek explained, my name sounding almost obscene coming from his mouth.

My head snapped up in time to see the sour look on Tasha's face, but my attention was swiftly brought back to Junior once he started coughing. When he grabbed his throat, I took off running up the stairs, quickly returning with his EpiPen and inhaler. Maleek looked panicked as he squatted next to Junior.

"Here, Junior," I said, placing the inhaler to his mouth after injecting the epinephrine into his right thigh muscle. "You know what to do."

Junior nodded as he depressed the trigger on the inhaler.

I scanned the kitchen. "Was any of this food cooked in peanut oil?"

Maleek looked up at me. "I don't know. Maybe the chicken on the chicken biscuits?"

"You gotta get them out of here."

He jumped to his feet, hurrying to the kitchen counter while saying, "Tasha, I need—"

"I ate it. All of it," she interrupted him.

"Good. Nuri, I'm sorry. This other one is yours," he said.

With my eyes glued to Junior, I responded, "It's okay. I already ate." Well, that was a lie, but whatever. "Throw it away outside the house."

"Got it."

I was trying to get a nap in before it was time to pick up the kids when my phone startled me awake. Seeing my new boss's name on the screen, I sat up, accepting the call with a coarse, "Hello?"

"Hey, were you sleep?" Maleek rumbled.

"No, I mean, yeah. A nap."

"My bad. We can talk later."

"No, it's okay. Did you need me to do something?"

"Nah, I just wanted to thank you again for helping Junior this morning and getting him to the ER. I can't believe he still wanted to go to school after all that."

"He likes school, and it was no problem. It's my job to do that stuff."

"Yeah...but you were incredible."

"Uh...thanks."

"You're welcome. Um, I found a pediatrician, got the kids an appointment for next Monday. I was wondering if you could go with us."

"Of course!"

"Cool. I'll see you later."

"Okay."

MALEEK

I don't know what brought me back to that McDonald's parking lot, but there I was, sitting in my Jeep, staring at her truck again. It was parked in the same spot as before on the hotel lot in the middle of the day. What was going on?

We'd just ended the call about the kids' doctor's appointment, and I watched as she opened the back driver's side door, stretching before pulling a pillow and blanket out of the backseat and walking around to the rear hatch. Frowning, I observed her digging through her stuff until she pulled out a toothbrush, toothpaste, and bottled water. Then she climbed into the driver's seat.

I was out of my vehicle and heading to hers before I realized what I was doing, making quick strides and swiftly finding myself knocking on her window. She jumped, her eyes wild as they collided with mine. Instead of letting the window down, she opened the door and hopped out of her truck.

"What the fuck?!" she shrieked.

"I dropped by this McDonald's on my way home from practice, noticed your car." So, that was a lie. The practice part was true, but this place was not on my route home from the arena.

"Oh...I...I'm..."

"Are you...do you live in this car, Nuri? Or at this hotel?"

Her response? Tears. She broke down right then and there, making my heart twist into a knot.

"Shit," I muttered, placing a hand on her shoulder. "Hey, I'm sorry. I didn't mean to upset you."

She dropped her head, sobbing, "You said you weren't the type to judge people!"

"I...I'm not." Instinctually, I pulled her toward me, wrapping her in my arms. She didn't resist, and the sensation of her soft body against mine felt...right. *So right.* Maybe *too* right. The next thing I knew, my dick was expanding because that motherfucker had a mind of his own. So, I ended the hug, cupping her face in my hands.

"Hey, I'm sorry. I'm not judging you. I wanna help you, if that's what you need," I offered.

She shook her head. "I don't need any help. Once I get paid, I'll be good. This is just a temporary issue, and it's not all that bad. I just haven't been sleeping well. It's hard to sleep in this thing, but I always try to park in safe areas."

I was speechless for a moment. She'd been sleeping in her truck?

She blinked, and another tear fell, staining her perfect brown skin.

Wiping it away, I blew out a breath. "Okay, how much you need to get a place?"

"I don't—"

"I realize you don't really know me, that we don't know each other, but I ain't the kind of nigga who can know some shit like this and do nothing. You ain't spending another night in this car. You can stay with us tonight. Tomorrow, I'll help you get a place."

"No, I can't stay with y'all. I...don't want to do that. I—your fiancée...I think she has enough to deal with right now."

I frowned. "What'd she say to you?"

"Nothing. Just...I can't do that."

I nodded. "A'ight, give me a minute to make a few calls. I'll be right back."

She gave me a confused look before saying, "Uh, sure?"

It only took me fifteen minutes to make my calls. When I was done, I dialed Nuri's number.

"Hello?" she answered.

"Hey, follow me," I said.

13

NURI

"Nuri Knox, this is Krystle Ford, the wife of—"

"*Ex*-wife," the tall chocolate-skinned woman amended, cutting Maleek off.

"Right, she's the *ex-wife* of one of my teammates. She's a real estate agent who specializes in luxury short-term rentals," he finished.

"Yes, and I think this place will be perfect for you. It's one bedroom, one bath, fully furnished," Krystle informed me.

I let my eyes round the small space. It was basically an upscale studio apartment.

"You think this'll be enough room for you? It *is* just you, right?" Maleek probed.

I nodded. "Uh, yeah. Just me. It's perfect. How much is the rent?"

"$1,500 per month, utilities included. The deposit is $800, or if you choose the month-to-month option, the owners will waive the deposit. The rent is slightly more in that case," Krystle advised.

It would take me less than a month to save the deposit and first month's rent, less time than that if I chose the second option, and after that, I'd be fine.

Maleek was staring at me, waiting for my answer, so I finally said, "I'd, um, need a couple weeks to raise the money. Can you hold it?"

"Nah, no waiting. I got you. I'm paying you today for the entire month," Maleek told me.

"What?" I peeped.

"Yeah, so you're spending the night here tonight, a'ight?" he said with lifted eyebrows.

Blinking back tears, I said. "All right."

After the whirlwind of a day I had once Maleek discovered my secret, my *shame*, I had to rush to pick the kids up, although he offered to take care of it so I could get settled in my place. I couldn't let him do that, not after he paid me four thousand dollars in cash for barely three days worth of work. I was so grateful that I spent most of the evening battling tears of pure happiness and appreciation.

I sniffled through cooking dinner and grinned like a complete fool every time I was in Maleek's presence. He seemed like such a great guy, so kind...and fine. When he hugged me, he smelled good, like soap and cologne and fine nigga pheromones. Did I have a crush on him? Probably, but crushes were harmless. He had a fiancée, and I wasn't one to pursue taken men, but I could look, fantasize, wish—

"Damn, it smells good in here!" his voice boomed from behind me. I was at the stove, a smile popping on my face the second I heard his voice.

Glancing over my shoulder at his tall frame, I said, "Thanks. Jules likes spaghetti, so I'm making some."

"Ah, she told you that?"

I gave him a smirk before we simultaneously said, "Junior."

I laughed and he beamed, his thick lips parting to reveal stark white teeth.

"My mom makes some bomb spaghetti. Can't wait to see how yours tastes," he shared.

"Oh, it's good," I assured him.

Licking his lips, he eyed me for a moment. "I bet it is."

Why was he giving me "fuck me" eyes? Shit!

"Um...so you're having dinner with the kids tonight?" I questioned.

"That's the plan, I want to try and have dinner with them every night I'm able to. Tryna get to know them better and stuff," he replied.

"Oh, okay. Well, there's plenty. Enough for Tasha, too."

"Word? I'll let her know."

About fifteen minutes later, the kids were sitting at the kitchen table devouring my spaghetti. So was Maleek, but no Tasha.

Thank. God.

I *really* didn't like her energy.

While they ate, I straightened up the kitchen, was in the middle of loading the dishwasher when I heard Maleek say, "You not gon' join us, Nuri?"

I turned to see him staring at me. "Oh, no. I'm good."

"So, you just not gonna eat dinner? That ain't good at all. Join us, Miss Knox."

I felt all gooey inside from him calling me Miss Knox. I was such a damn simp, but simp or not, I *was* hungry, so I fixed myself a plate and took a seat at the table directly across from Maleek.

"Y'all like your new school?" he asked the kids.

Both kids gave him a nod but neither spoke since their mouths were full.

Maleek chuckled. "Y'all tearing this food up. It's good, though. Real good."

I looked up from my plate to see that his appreciative eyes were on me.

So, I said, "Thanks."

"You need help moving into your place?" he asked me.

"I don't think so since it's furnished. I was planning on leaving my big items in storage for now and just moving in my clothes, personal items, stuff like that," I answered.

"I got you, but if you decide you do need some help, let me know."

"I will."

MALEEK

I was lying in bed, my mind full of so much shit that it felt like it would explode. We had a game tomorrow, and Junior had asked if he and Jules could see me play. Of course, I said yes, and Nuri quickly offered to bring them, though that wasn't in her job description. She reminded me of my mom in a lot of ways—sweet, caring, but unlike my mom, she did have some self-preservation. She'd refused to stay at the house with us, and I knew it was because of Tasha.

The woman I was going to marry wouldn't even attempt to get to know my siblings and pretty much acted like Nuri didn't exist. I was trying to work with her because I really did understand why she was upset, but shit! This was a lot on me, too! I needed her support, even if she faked it. I didn't need any more stuff to deal with, but I was going to ride it out. I supposed I owed it to her since she'd always been my ride or die, never missing a game, willing to deal with me splitting my attention between her and hockey, coping with my awkwardness early on. Yeah, I owed her.

"Are those your kids?"

Frowning, I turned my head to see Tasha's back, the screen of her cell providing the only light in our bedroom. "What?"

"Are those your kids?" she repeated matter-of-factly.

I sat up against the headboard, reaching to turn the lamp on. "Tash, look at me."

"Answer the question, Maleek."

"If you want to ask me some insulting shit like that, you need to look me in the face and do it."

She flipped over, one eyebrow raised. "Are. Those. Your. Kids?"

"Hell. Fucking. No. Jules is seven. I've been with you for seven damn years! Are you serious right now?!"

"Dead serious. None of this makes sense! All I ever heard you say about your father was how he dumped you and you have turned our lives upside down for his kids!"

"Tash! You were there. You heard the social worker. Those kids were in the system. They don't have anyone else! It ain't their fault our father was an asshole to me, and they're good kids. They haven't been any trouble."

She shook her head for the entirety of my response. "Nope, I'm not buying it. You always complained about your mom letting people use her, and you're doing the same thing!"

"What?! Who is using me? The kids?"

"Your father!"

"My father is dead!"

"Yeah, and despite abandoning you, he listed you as their guardian. It was like he knew you'd go along with it. Maybe that's because all that shit you told me was a lie, and all this time, he was raising some kids you had by a white girl. Pretending you were a virgin when we got together? *That* was crazy."

I stared at her before saying, "I'm not doing this. You wanna believe that stupid shit? Then believe it. I got a long day tomorrow, a game tomorrow night, and I need sleep."

"So that's it?"

"Tash, I love you—"

"But do you, Maleek?"

I don't know, I thought, but said, "I'm going to sleep."

"That's not an answer."

"Goodnight, Tash," I said, turning the lamp off and settling into my side of the bed.

·　·　·

Early the next morning, I stood at the toilet emptying my bladder, my mind still foggy. My heart was in a tangle. One of my hands rested on the wall above the toilet, the other holding my dick. I needed more sleep, but my bed felt inhospitable after the previous night's argument. Maybe I'd crash on the sofa for an hour before starting my day.

"I'm sorry." Her voice made me jump a little in addition to cutting my stream off. "Damn, Tash...you scared the shit out of me!"

"I didn't mean to," she offered.

I finished pissing, flushed, and washed my hands before turning to face her. She was naked, standing in the bathroom doorway, her bottom lip tucked between her teeth.

Slowly, she inched toward me, placing her hands on my bare chest. "Do you forgive me?"

"Tash—"

"I apologize, bae. I'm just...I was being stupid. I guess all the changes, the stress, it's getting to me and making me crazy. It's only been a few days. I'll adjust. I love you, Maleek. You're my forever."

Then she kissed me, and I kissed her back.

14

"You left my place and haven't called me since. I know my cats are tyrants but damn, Nuri!" Coco shrieked into the phone. I'd known her since fifth grade, and I loved her from the hair she kept dyed purple to her polka-dotted toenails, but I'd been going through it, and she knew it.

"You can't cut me some slack while I'm going through shit? My aunt, your cats, all that?" I asked.

"I just took accountability for the cats. Look, I'm worried about you! Where've you been staying? Did you get another job? Are you okay?"

Rolling over in bed in my new home, I smiled. "I'm good. Got a job as a nanny for this hockey player. The pay is great, and I got a new place."

"A nanny? Really?"

"Yeah, and the kids are sweet. The boss is nice. It's been great so far."

"What's the hockey player's name?"

"Uh, Maleek Jones. He plays for the Sires."

"Okay..." I knew she was Googling him. "Oh, he's black!"

"Duh. I said his name is *Maleek Jones*."

"Shit! Nuri, this man is fine as hell! Wait, he has a fiancée. She's cute. They make a good couple."

"They really do."

"Yeah, but how do you keep from drooling over him? Like, damn!"

"I just wait until I'm not around him to drool, but I definitely drool. He's the finest man I've ever laid eyes on. Hands down, but that's all it is—me drooling."

"Baybeee, being in his presence has got to provide months worth of masturbation material. Wow!"

"Yep. Hey, I'm taking the kids to his game tonight. Wanna come with? I have an extra ticket."

"Absolutely! I've never been to a hockey game before."

"Me either."

The arena was kind of cold. I knew it would be because Maleek told me to be sure to bundle the kids and myself up. Plus, it made sense. They had to keep the ice cold, but got damn! It was *arctic* where we were sitting.

Maleek initially wanted us to sit in the WAGs box with Tasha because he was afraid something would trigger Junior's allergy or asthma, but Junior begged to sit in the arena to be close to the action. He won. Armed with an EpiPen and his inhaler, here we were.

"It's cold as hell in here," Coco said, echoing my thoughts.

"Yeah," I agreed.

Maleek said the seats he got us were good because they were against the glass. I had no idea what that meant until we arrived and I saw that only a pane of plexiglass separated us from the action on the ice. Evidently, it also meant we'd be colder than in other parts of the arena.

"I heard there's a room where the wives who sit out here can go get wine and stuff between periods. There's also space for their kids to play in there," Coco said. "Wonder if it's warmer in there?"

"Who told you that? Mr. Google?"

"Yep."

"It'll get warmer when all the people get in here," Junior advised us.

I smiled down at him in his new black jacket and skull cap. "That makes sense."

"Yeah. I wish I could ride the Zamboni. I always wanted to do that," Junior informed me.

"Not me," Jules said with wide eyes, making me laugh.

"What's a Zamboni?" I asked Junior.

"It's a machine that cleans the ice and stuff like that. You'll see! Can we get food? Hockey game food is the best!" Junior informed me once we settled in our seats. He and Jules seemed oblivious to the cold. "Jules wants nachos. I want pizza."

"How do you know this stuff about hockey games?" I queried.

"Our dad took us to one in Nashville one time. He hardly ever did stuff with us, so I remember."

"You didn't get to spend much time with your dad?" I asked.

Junior shook his head. "No, our mom, either."

Not wanting to pry too much, I said, "Okay...nachos and pizza it is."

"I'll go get it," Coco offered.

Digging the money Maleek had given me for the game out of my purse, I handed some to her. "Thanks, Co."

She left, and when I wasn't watching the kids' reactions to everything from the people filing into the massive space to the blue and red lines, circles, markings, and Sires logo on the ice, or rather, underneath the ice, I took in my surroundings. I'd never been the biggest sports fan other than watching the occasional NBA game. I knew nothing at all about hockey, but I guessed I was about to learn.

Music had been filling the arena since we arrived. Now they were playing Nelly's *Hot in Herre*, which made me smile since I was anything but hot where we were sitting, even with my jacket on. *I should've worn gloves.*

Glancing at the kids, I smiled again. Evidently, they both arrived in St. Louis with Sires jerseys emblazoned with their big brother's name and number on them.

"Where'd y'all get those jerseys?" I asked whichever one of them wanted to answer. Surprisingly, it was Jules who replied.

"Our dad got them for us last Christmas. They were too big then but now they fit," she said in a voice so soft I barely heard her over the music that had changed to Britney Spears' *Toxic*.

"Oh, nice!" I responded.

"Yeah. He really liked Maleek. He talked about him all the time," Junior interjected.

I nodded. "Really? That's good," but I had to wonder why Maleek was just now meeting them. Had their father kept the three of them separate? They obviously had different mothers. I quickly told myself to stop thinking about that stuff. My job was to care for these kids, not meddle. I didn't want to ask or say the wrong thing and end up sleeping in my car and taking ho' baths in various public restrooms again.

By the time Coco made it back with the food, the lights had been dimmed, *King of Rock* was blasting at the highest decibel, and the crowd was losing its mind.

It was game time.

Hockey is brutal and fast-paced and exciting! From the puck-drop onward, the only words to describe the action out on the ice were *pure adrenaline*. It was hard for me to follow at first, but little Junior gave me a great tutorial. The main thing he taught me was to follow the puck. That tiny little black thing was the center of attraction, and getting it past the opponent's goalie and into the netted goal was the main objective. Once I got that, I almost understood what was happening. I tried to stay focused on the puck but there was so much going on, like the players changing out what felt like every few seconds, creating chaotically rhythmic traffic on the ice, players elbowing each other, players running into the walls, players knocking each other into the walls *and* the glass. Yes, the glass! The whole thing shook when that happened, scaring the shit out of me until I got used to it. Sitting at the glass was like being on the ice! One player actually snatched a guy's stick from him, and there was a fight, a whole-ass fight between two opposing players, but neither was Maleek, who, by the way, could skate his ass off, but I suppose that was a job requirement. He was fast on those things, too, and he could work the shit out of that puck with his stick. He was so...skilled and agile. It was kind of sexy.

Scratch that, it was *extremely* sexy.

And he was fine as hell in that hockey gear.

At one point, Maleek ended up in the penalty box, which Junior said is kind of like hockey jail, but he was only in there for a few minutes. I guess that whole process was like getting a foul in basketball...maybe? It was interesting, though. All in all, despite my confusion, I enjoyed the game. The energy was crazy, the fans were rabid, and seeing Mr. Maleek Jones in action was exhilarating, since I was coming to the realization that in just a few days of knowing him, I'd developed a huge crush on him. That was no good since he had a fiancée, but the crazy thing was that I got these vibes from him, vibes that he liked me, too.

MALEEK

"It was so good! I wanna go to all the games!" Junior gushed as we sat at the breakfast table the morning after the game.

I glanced at Nuri, who was at the kitchen counter fixing the kids' plates. "Well, if Nuri's okay with it, you can come to some more home games, but not all of them. That would be a lot, and she has to have some off days. Plus, you guys have school. Can't be out late all the time."

"Awwwww," they both whined. I smiled at hearing Jules' soft voice.

Placing plates in front of them, Nuri said, "I don't mind taking them to as many of the home games as you'd like me to. It was... different. Violent, but interesting. You wanna plate, Maleek?"

"Yeah, I'll fix my own," I replied, following her to the counter. "Hey, we really do need to discuss off days for you. You want the weekends off?"

She frowned, leaning against the counter next to me as I piled bacon, eggs, and biscuits onto my plate. "Junior told me you play a lot of games. Don't you play on the weekend sometimes?"

I looked up at her. Wrong move. The expression on her face—wrinkled brow, long lashes low, mouth twisted to the side, arms folded under her breasts—all of that made her look too damn cute. "Uh...I...yeah," I stammered.

"Then who's going to watch them if I'm off? You got backup?"

Damn, she had a point.

"Uh...I'll figure it out. You can't work every day," I muttered, grabbing the back of my neck.

Kids were stressful as fuck.

"Oh, and Junior mentioned something about riding the Zamboni? That's the truck looking thing I saw out on the ice, right? Is he allowed to do that at his age?" she questioned.

"Yeah, he's old enough. I'll check into it for him," I said.

She smiled at me, and my damn heart inexplicably melted. "Okay, thanks!" she chirped

I was tired, too tired to even consider having this conversation with Tasha, but it had to be done.

I was fresh out the shower, having just arrived home after practice, when I decided to get it over with. After a quick search of the house, I found her in the living room curled up on the sofa and scrolling through Instagram on her phone. The kids were at school and Nuri was off doing whatever she did when she wasn't with them. The house was quiet, which heightened my anxiety as I plopped down beside her, placing a hand on her thigh.

She looked up at my face, a smile spreading across hers. "Hey! You smell good."

"Thanks, uh...can I ask you something?"

She adjusted herself until she was leaning into me. Kissing me softly on the lips, she nodded. "Of course, baby. What's up?"

I cleared my throat, dropping my eyes from her pretty face to the floor. "You know we got that game in NYC on Saturday, right?"

"Yep! Me and my girls are gonna watch it here. "

"Yeah, so...I was thinking, Nuri gotta have some off days, you know? So, you think you could watch the kids Saturday? You know they gon' fly us back that night, so I got them on Sunday."

She sighed, shaking her head. "Maleek, you gotta send those kids back."

"Back where?! To the state? To foster care? I'm all they got, Tash! You know that!"

"I'm sure there's some really nice couple somewhere who'd love to adopt them. They're big, too big for us to be trying to raise, and none of this, and I mean, *none of this* makes sense! You are making sacrifices, stressing both you and me out, and hemorrhaging money for some kids you don't know just because you have the same father, a father who never gave half a shit about you? What are you doing?"

"The right thing."

"The right thing for who?"

"Them!"

"What about you? Me? *Us?!* I love you, Maleek, I really do, but I didn't sign up for this shit!" She was on her feet now, her voice loud and shrill.

"Neither did I! I didn't plan this, Tash, but I'm doing what feels right in my heart. That's it. I'm not trying to hurt or inconvenience you. I'll...I'll see if Nuri knows someone who can be her backup."

She closed her eyes and blew out a breath. "How long do you plan on doing this? Is this permanent? Do you actually plan on raising these kids?"

"I don't know. Maybe."

"Maleek, I can't do this. I can't..." Her voice was soft, almost defeated.

Silence crowded the open space of the living room before I finally said, "I'm sorry, Tash, but..."

"But what?" she snapped.

I fixed my eyes on her face. "But I understand. I really do. This is a lot. I don't expect you to shoulder all this."

"So, you're good with me leaving you, ending things?"

"No, I'm not. I just...I get it, Tash."

"So that's it? This is the end?"

"If that's what you want."

She scoffed, "What *I* want? I think this is what *you* want, Maleek. I think it's what you wanted all along."

She pushed past me, leaving me standing there battling with a deep sense of guilt and a deeper feeling of relief.

By the time the kids were home from school, Tasha had packed a couple bags and left, informing me that she'd be back for the rest of her things soon. The kids were in the kitchen eating a snack when I approached Nuri whose wide eyes and bright smile made me feel even worse about what I needed to ask of her.

"Hey, I know you're not really settled into your new place yet, but..."

15

NURI

He asked me to move in, as in move into this...mansion of his. Tasha was gone, and although he didn't share the details of why she left, I figured it had a lot to do with Jules and Junior, and while I didn't like her all that much, I understood her plight. She was with Maleek because she wanted *him*. The kids were additions she was not expecting and was ill-prepared for. Children were a lot to adjust to even when they were expected. Unexpected, they could turn one's life completely upside down. I knew because I'd been one of those unexpected kids, but my matriarchs—my mom, followed by my grandmother—had loved me and treated me like a gift, a treasure, and I missed them both.

Anyway, there I was, adjusting to another new, possibly impermanent home. This had now been my address for three days. I wondered how many more days would pass before that changed. According to Maleek, he was granted emergency guardianship but wasn't sure what the future held beyond that, so who knew how long this gig would last? As I sat in the living room, my eyes glued to the huge photo of Maleek and Tasha displayed on the wall, I also realized they were likely to reunite, which would most certainly mean I'd have to move out. See, nothing was certain, and while I should've been accustomed to the insecurity I'd been existing in for months, I wasn't. I was worried and afraid and cautious.

Dropping my eyes to the silver and white leopard print rug on the floor, I told myself that at least my pay was the same and I wasn't being charged room and board. Therefore, I could save virtually every penny I made, stockpile funds for the inevitable next alteration in my life. I'd continue to pay the rent on my apartment, of course. I wasn't trying to end up homeless again.

It was late, and after watching the Sires game on the Black Sports Network with me, the kids had gone to bed. I was contemplating doing the same when I heard the front door open. It was too early for Maleek to be back.

Did I forget to lock it? I wondered.

I froze, expecting the alarm to start blaring, hoping it would send whoever it was running, but that didn't happen. Instead, I heard the distinct sound of the buttons being pressed on the panel by the door. Whoever this was knew the code. It had to be Maleek, but how'd he make it back so early?

I blew out the breath I'd been holding and relaxed before leaving the sofa and making my way to the foyer to greet him and give him my regrets on the team's loss.

"Hey? You're bac—" I stopped when I saw her—puffy eyes, a hoodie hiding her hair.

Tasha.

"Oh...I thought you were Maleek," I said.

She rolled her eyes. "Yeah, well...I need to pick up a few things. I'll be gone before he gets back, I'm sure."

"Okay," I uttered softly as she began ascending the stairs.

MALEEK

Dragging myself through the door, I dropped my duffel on the floor and quickly plugged the code into the alarm keypad. Then I stood there, taking in the quiet, the peace, the absence of the pain I should've felt about my woman of damn near a decade leaving me. Instead, it was like this invisible pressure that'd been weighing on me had lifted.

"Oh, it's you. Good," a soft voice said.

I looked up to see Nuri standing near the bottom of the stairs in pink shorts, a red and white t-shirt that resembled one of those plastic, white Chinese take-out bags—it even said "thank you"—a pink bonnet, and fuzzy pink slippers.

"You were expecting someone else?" I asked, mentally adding, *like your boyfriend?*

Soooo, I had no idea where that thought came from. Maybe the fact that she looked so cute, cute and sexy, had something to do with it. Even that damn bonnet was cute.

"No, I just...Tasha dropped by earlier. I mean, it was late but earlier than now," she stated.

I frowned. "She did?"

Nodding, she affirmed, "Yes, she did."

"Did she...did she say anything to you?"

"Just that she was picking up a few things. She was in and out."

"She let herself in?"

"Yes."

"A'ight. Well, sorry I woke you up."

"You didn't. I'm...trying to adjust to living here. Haven't been sleeping well."

"Sorry...*again.*"

"Don't be. Hey, sorry about the game. You did good, though."

I smiled, kind of tickled at her assessment of my performance. "You think so? Thanks."

"Yeah, and you jacked that one dude up. He hit the wall hard!"

Now I was smiling wider. "When you're skating that fast, hard hits are pretty much inevitable."

"I bet. I've always wanted to learn how to ice skate."

"Really? Then I'll have to teach you."

"That'd be great. Do you get cold out there on the ice? I was wondering about that."

"Nah, the game is too fast paced; we're basically constantly moving and have on all that gear. Half the time, I'm sweating out there."

"Wow! Well, I know you've got to be tired. I'll let you go to bed."

"Tired, sore, banged up, you name it, but I'm used to it."

"Yeah. So...see you in the morning?"

"Yeah...good night, Nuri."

"Good night."

Me: *Hey*

An hour later and no response from Tasha. So, I texted her again.

Me: *Tash...*

Her: *What?*

I could hear the attitude in that text.

Me: *How are you?*

Her: *Wonderful. Great. I love living with my mom again.*

I scratched my forehead before typing my response: *I'm sorry.*

Her: *Yeah.*

Me: *Look, I just wanted to ask that you let me know before you come get the rest of your stuff so I can be here.*

Her: *Why do you need to be there? Did Nora complain or something?*

Me: *Nuri.*

Her: *Yeah. That.*

Me: *No. I'd just like to be here.*

She never replied to my last text.

———

"She left?! You're lying!"

I rolled my eyes at Ford's loud ass. "I'm not lying, and do you think you can get any louder? I'm sure folks outside the arena can hear you."

"My bad, but damn! Y'all been together forever. I just can't believe this shit. I thought you two were solid," he responded using his inside voice.

"We were. It was the kids. They were too much for her, and I understand where she's coming from."

"Yeah, kids ain't no joke. It's been a couple weeks since you got them, right? So...this is permanent? You keeping the kids, I mean."

I shrugged. "I'm all they got."

"Damn, that's tough, man. The secret nanny still working out?"

"Yeah, she's great. She basically moved in after Tasha left. I gotta find someone to take up the slack so she can get some off days. She don't complain about the hours, though, and the kids love her."

Ford smiled at me. "I see you still ain't dropped her name, which means she's stacked with a donkey ass, ain't she? She ain't up in that new house nannying your dick, is she?"

"My woman just left me, and you think I'm tryna fuck somebody?"

"A fine somebody? Yep."

"I ain't you, Loose Dick McGee."

"Fuck you, Jones. You and Rapp act like y'all ain't never fucked up."

"That's because we haven't, Ford," Rapp cut in.

"Good game, my brothers. We'll get them next time! Uhhhhh, nah-nah-nah-nahhhh!" Robin Stick bellowed Master P style, offering Ford some dap as he exited the locker room. We'd lost another game, a *home* game. That shit always sucked. That was why I was hanging around the locker room for so long. I didn't have the energy or the heart to leave just yet.

"Did Stick have a durag on?" Rapp asked. "He gotta stop."

Ford laughed, and I shook my head.

"So, Jones...Sexy Nanny brought the kids to the game tonight, didn't she? You gon' let me meet her?" Ford asked, rubbing his hands together.

"*Hell* naw," I growled.

NURI

"How old are you, Miss Nuri?" Junior asked through a mouthful of corn. I looked up from my plate to see him holding the half-eaten cob in his hands. Then I scanned the rest of the table, my eyes colliding with the expectant gazes of Jules and Maleek.

"First, no talking with your mouth full. Second, why do you want to know, Little Mister?" I answered.

"Because I know that Jules is seven and I'm ten and Maleek is twenty-six. How old are you?"

Twenty-six? I thought. Didn't Coco tell me she read somewhere that he was twenty-eight?

"You're twenty-six?" I queried, my eyes fixed on Maleek.

Chewing, he locked eyes with me and nodded.

Wow! So young to be so...mature, responsible, sexy as hell.

"Well, if you must know, I'm thirty-one," I divulged.

"Ohhhh, that's old!" Junior yelled.

With wide eyes, I protested, "No it's not!"

"Man, it's rude to ask a lady her age," Maleek said.

"Why?" Junior chirped.

"It just is, and thirty-one ain't old. Besides, Nuri doesn't look thirty-one. At all," Maleek responded, his attention on me again.

"How old does she look?" Junior interrogated.

"I don't know...maybe twenty-six," Maleek said, smiling at me.

In return, I swear my pussy purred in appreciation.

. . .

Hey, cuz! Just checking on you. Everything good? Mama said you were looking for a place to stay. Did you ever find one?

I stared at the message from my cousin Terry and shook my head. At that point, it'd been more than a month since I made the call to his mother, three weeks since I'd been working for Maleek Jones, and he was just now contacting me?

Asshole.

I ignored the message, resuming my current project. Maleek had ordered more furniture for the kids' rooms, and I was in Jules' room assembling her off-white-colored dresser. It was too cute with butterfly drawer pulls.

"Need some help?"

I jumped at the unexpected sound of Maleek's voice, slapping a hand over my heart. Turning to face him, I screeched, "OMG, you scared me!"

"My bad, Miss Thirty-one," he apologized. "That still blows my mind. You look much younger."

"Thank you," I said, sounding timid for some unknown reason.

"You're welcome. So...do you?"

"Do I what?"

"Need some help?"

"Oh! Sure!"

We sat on the floor, working quietly for a while save for discussing what went where and who would hold what until he just started talking: "The kids seem to be adjusting well. They're doing great in school. They seem happy. It's kind of weird. Like, I'm a complete stranger to them and they act like this has always been their home. This whole transition has been easy, *mad* easy."

"I think that's because of you. You've never made them feel like they didn't belong here or with you," I said.

"You might be right."

"I *am* right."

He grinned. "Anyway, they just go with the flow, you know? I told them about Tasha leaving and they didn't bat an eye."

"Well...I mean, she wasn't exactly...uh..."

"I know, I know. She...uh...struggled with this...change."

"Struggled is a good word."

Chuckling, he twirled the screwdriver he was holding. "Anyway, I...this all feels strange. They never mention their parents. At all. They don't really seem all that sad. I...I still don't know them, not really. I don't know what life was like for them before. They're great kids. I just wish Jules would talk more."

"Therapy will help with all that. They lost both their parents. I'm sure that's impacted them. I *know* it has."

"Yeah. You're still going to the therapist with us, right?"

I nodded. "Of course."

"Thanks. I appreciate that," he stated.

"You already met with her, right? Told her about them?"

"Yeah, I had to squeeze that meeting in, but I made it happen."

"Good."

"Yeah," he agreed. Then he just stared at me, and I stared at him. Maleek was rarely home, always at practice or a game or a meeting. When he *was* home, he really tried to bond with his siblings and help me with household tasks. He was kind, conscientious, and so damn sexy. It was hard for me not to sneak looks at him, but now, I was out-and-out staring. So was he, and it didn't feel awkward. It felt...right.

"Nuri," he said, his voice deep and thick. Twenty-six? Well, he had the spirit and aura of a forty-year-old zaddy. I swear, I was falling in love with this man.

Real bad.

"Yes?" I squealed.

"I—thank you for everything. You're so good with the kids. I just...I don't know what I'd do without your help."

"I like the kids. I...you're welcome."

"Nuri, I lik—"

Ding-dong!

The doorbell.

He blinked and shook his head. "Let me go get that."

I gave him a nod and watched him leap to his feet and leave the room.

16

MALEEK

I opened the door, the chilly air whipping my bare legs in my basketball shorts. Before I could say a word, she lit into me.

"You changed the fucking locks?!" Tasha screamed. "You changed the locks, restricting my access to my own fucking home?!"

"You left," I replied.

"And you obviously don't give a fuck! You have not once come to visit me, called me, nothing! Just a dumb-ass text about letting you know before I come to *my* house!"

"Tash—"

"And I bet those kids are still living here, aren't they?!" She said that shit as if she was catching me in a lie or something.

"I never definitively said they were going anywhere, Tasha. This is their home now." I hadn't raised my voice...*yet*, but she was going to have to calm the-fuck down.

"So, you really chose them over me! Seven years! Seven fucking years of my life wasted on a nigga I had to teach how to fuck!"

"Okay."

"Okay?! Everything is always *okay* with you, isn't it?!"

"Tash—"

"You know what? Sell this house. I deserve half of what it's worth. I picked it out, decorated it. It's mine!"

I stared at this beautiful woman, dressed head to toe in expensive clothes I paid for. Hell, she drove here in a car *I* bought. She still had my credit cards and was using them.

Shaking my head, I told her, "We aren't married, and my name is the only one on this house. I'm not selling it and uprooting those kids any more than they already have been. Now, why are you here? To get the rest of your stuff? If so, you're more than welcome to do that now, while the kids are at school." I'd just finished my statement when I sensed, rather than saw, Nuri.

Turning from where Tasha still stood in the open doorway, I spotted Nuri standing at the bottom of the staircase in her light blue sweatsuit, her braids—a fresh 'do some chick had done in my kitchen—were piled on top of her head and her lips were shiny like she had just put on some gloss or something.

Too cute.

"Uh...it's time for me to go pick the kids up," Nuri said softly. I don't think I'd ever once heard her raise her voice. She was so damn chill. All the time, chill.

I nodded, turning to see Tasha still standing in the doorway, her head swinging from me to Nuri and back. "What? I'm in the way?"

"Actually, yes," I said.

She stepped inside, crowding my personal space, her eyes narrowed as she turned to Nuri. She opened her mouth to say something, but I preempted her.

"Go ahead, Nuri," I stated.

Nuri had barely made it out the door when Tasha shrieked, "Are you fucking her?! *Her?!*"

"No, and why you gotta say it like that?"

"Look at her! She's fat!"

"A'ight, it's time for you to go. I'll send your stuff to your mom's."

"I know the-fuck you are not putting me out because I called that girl fat!"

"No!" I shouted, making her flinch. I rarely raised my voice, but this was stupid. *She* left *me* and was over here acting like it was the other way around. "I'm putting you out because this is *my* house, and you don't live here anymore. You left, moved out. We're no longer together and I'm not tryna deal with you yelling and shit, especially when the kids will be home soon."

She backed away from me and threw up her hands. "The kids. The got damn kids! You know what, Maleek? Fuck you *and* those kids!" With that, she left.

I'm sorry. I shouldn't have acted like that earlier. I shouldn't have insinuated that you were fucking that chubby girl. I know better. I just miss you, Maleek. I miss **us**. *Look, I'm going on vacation with my mom. We're going to Paris. When we get back, maybe me and you can sit down and talk, try to fix things. We've got too much history to just throw it all away. I love you.*

I finished reading the text from Tasha and refocused on Jules, who was doing a great job of coloring the sheet full of African American inventors.

———

"I haven't heard from you since I was discharged. Everything okay? How are the kids? Little Jules still not talking?"

I had to smile at hearing my mom's voice, a reliable source of comfort for me. "My bad, Ma. Things have been hectic. The kids are good, adjusting well. Jules still doesn't say much, but we've got therapy coming up. Hopefully, that'll help us get to the bottom of that."

"Hmm, I bet things *are* hectic. I'd love to meet the kids. I need to see you, too."

"I know, Ma. I'ma make it happen. I promise."

"How's Tasha been handling everything? This is a huge change, can't be easy for her."

I sighed into the phone. It was crazy to me that my mom would bother to show concern for a woman she barely knew. We might have been together for seven years, but Tasha kept her interactions with my mom to a bare minimum. I didn't push her because...hell, I don't know why. Maybe I was embarrassed of my mom's issues, and that would make me pretty much a shitty person.

"She left," I admitted. "Said it was too much."

"Oh, I'm sorry, Poo. How are you dealing with the breakup?"

"I get it. It's a lot. I understand her decision."

"That's not what I asked you, son."

Silence from me. I was ashamed to admit how I truly felt about it.

"Did I ever tell you how me and your father broke up?" she asked.

"No, ma'am," I replied, sinking deeper into the driver's seat of my vehicle.

"I think you were two or three, and we were living in this tiny house in Memphis over on Kippley. Your father loved me the best way he knew how. He was always...well, you know."

"He was always about himself," I interjected.

"Yes, but he provided for us, and we were good for a time. Then I realized I didn't like him. I *loved* him, but I didn't like the person he was. I also realized he wasn't going to change, so I decided I couldn't go on pretending. Poo-bear, life was hard after I left him. You know this. It would've been much easier to stay, but I would've never been happy with him, and despite my battles with my mental health, I'm happy more days than not. I freed myself from him, but sometimes, when we don't have the strength to do it, to free ourselves, the other party will do it for us. Ain't no shame in being relieved about it."

I nodded, my eyes focused out the windshield on the huge building before me. "Thanks for that, Ma. Uh...I need to get off. Got practice and a game tonight."

"Okay, one more thing. Now that she's freed you, don't let that people-pleasing spirit I passed on to you make you trap yourself again."

"Yes, ma'am."

"Juh-Juh-Juh-G Unit!" Robin Stick yelled, rushing up on me and grabbing my helmet while I was sitting in the locker room, my stick in hand. At the last minute, I was trying to be sure my tape was on point. It was one of my game day rituals. The last-minute part, I mean. If nothing else, Stick knew how to hype the team up on game nights, even if it was by yelling out random Black shit. His ass swore he was a part of the diaspora.

"Yeah!!!! Let's get it, Sires!" Ford shouted as I followed him out of the locker room into the tunnel where *Southern Comfort* always did our ritualistic handshake, the cameras catching it all for the fans both at home and in the arena via the Jumbotron. When I heard our intro music being played—*King of Rock* by Run DMC—I knew the lights were dancing throughout the arena. That's when the adrenaline kicked in. By the time my name was announced and I was out on the ice, my stick in hand, the sound of the crowd cheering filling my ears, I was pumped all the way up. There was nothing like that shit!

Yeah, hockey was truly my first love.

NURI

You're going to burn your clit off if you don't stop.

That thought echoed in my head as I sat on the side of my bed and tore the package open. I'd made a trip to a sex shop while the kids were at school and was now holding a brand-new rose vibrator thingy because living in this house with this fine man was going to make me lose my mind. It wasn't that he did anything overtly sexual. The man was effortlessly sexy. When he ate—sexy. When he smiled —sexy. When he did absolutely nothing—sexy! He was also my boss, and I needed to keep my job. I could not fuck this up by accidentally offering him some pussy no matter how badly I wanted to, *and* he was engaged. Sure, she'd left. I heard them argue the other day, but they were together for years. Undoubtedly, they'd get back together. So...the rose. I was going to put this toy to work, relieve some pressure, and I'd be fine.

"Hello?" I answered my phone as I pulled into the pickup line at Sebayt House. I liked the small campus from the neat lawn to the brick buildings freshly painted black.

"Hey...Nuri?" It was definitely my Aunt Yvette. I thought I was tripping when I saw her name pop up on my phone's screen.

"Yes, it's me," I replied.

"Oh, you sound different. Anyway, I'm just calling to see what you're bringing to Thanksgiving this year. We're having it at Mother Dear's house, as usual."

Mother Dear, my sweet grandmother.

Sigh.

"Um...I haven't thought about it. I wasn't sure if I was still welcome."

"You're family. Of course, you're welcome."

I held the phone.

"Nuri?"

"I've made other arrangements for Thanksgiving this year. Can't make it."

I heard her sigh into the phone. "You're upset because I didn't let you move into my mother's house? You still need somewhere to stay or something?"

"I gotta go, Auntie. Goodbye."

I ended the call just as Jules and Junior approached my truck, hand in hand.

17

MALEEK

D r. Keyonna Rice was a psychologist who specialized in grief counseling for children. She came highly recommended, and her fee was hefty. I hoped she'd be a good fit for Junior and Jules.

I'd already met with her to discuss the kids—Jules' voluntarily limited speech, what I knew of their parents' deaths, and how they'd been adjusting to living with me. I also shared with her that the judge had okayed my guardianship, my *permanent* guardianship. That was a fact I hadn't shared with anyone else. Not even my mom. I told her about Nuri—our angel. I divulged how I was finding it hard to balance everything and how I worked so much that a month in, I still didn't really know my siblings. She recommended that *I* get therapy.

What the fuck?

And *hell* no!

This wasn't about me. I didn't need a damn thing but maybe some pussy. I missed pussy. Anyway, Dr. Rice wanted me there for the entire first session. After that, we'd see how comfortable the kids were with seeing her alone. So, there I sat, feeling awkward as hell and wishing Nuri was in there with us instead of waiting in the lobby as I watched the kids draw pictures. That was it. Dr. Rice told them to draw whatever they wanted. I was trying to trust the process, but damn! This was one expensive-ass art class.

"Junior, are you ready to show me and Maleek what you drew?" Dr. Rice asked several minutes into the session.

Junior nodded, holding up his drawing. It was a kitchen with two people sitting at a table with bowls before them. "This is me and my sister before our mom and dad died."

"Oh, I see," Dr. Rice began, "but where are your mom and dad?"

"Gone. They went on a date, so I fixed me and Jules some cereal for dinner."

"How old are you in this picture?"

He shrugged. "Ummmmm, eight. Jules was five."

Damn, I thought.

"How does this drawing make you feel, Junior?" Dr. Rice questioned.

He shrugged again. "Like a grown up because I was in charge. I wasn't scared like I was the first time I had to babysit Jules."

Dr. Rice gave him a smile. "Thank you for sharing that with us, Junior. Jules, can we see your picture?"

Jules nodded, holding up her drawing. I couldn't make it out, though. It looked like she just scribbled all over the paper. That was odd because I'd seen Jules draw and color better than that.

"Do you want to tell us what you made, Jules?" Dr. Rice asked her.

Without hesitation, Jules whispered, "Me."

"Where are you in this picture? Can you show us?" the doctor probed.

"I'm hiding in this picture," Jules explained.

Glancing at me, Dr. Rice asked, "Hiding from what?"

Jules shrugged. "Mommy and Daddy. They're fighting."

. . .

I basically stumbled up the front steps, fumbled for my keys, and felt like collapsing when I finally made it inside my house. It was a game day, and after our morning practice, I had to sit through a team meeting and then take a call with Nate. I was tired as all fuck and planned to nap until just before it was time for me to leave for the game.

After making a quick trip to the kitchen to down a snack, I inched up the stairs, passing the closed doors of the kids' and Nuri's rooms on my way to the master suite. Nuri's Explorer was in the driveway, so I figured she was getting a nap in, too. I kind of wanted to knock on her door anyway, just to see her face and maybe chat for a second, but she definitely deserved her rest, so I wasn't going to disturb her.

I'd just passed her door when I heard her say something. I stopped, strained my ears, heard nothing, and shook my head. Was exhaustion making me hear shit now?

I'd taken one step toward my room when I heard it again—a grunting or straining sound, then a shriek, like a pained or frightened shriek.

Turning, I knocked on her door. "Nuri?!"

"Ahhhhhh!" she screamed, and that's when I kicked the door in, which was followed by another scream. The darkness of the room disoriented me. It was the middle of the day and almost pitch black with the heavy curtains closed and the lights off. It was so dark, and that smell—pussy. It definitely smelled like pussy, *good* pussy. There was a buzzing coming from somewhere, too, and just beneath that noise was heavy breathing.

What the fuck?

"Oh my god! What are you doing in here?!" she yelled.

Snapping out of my confusion, my eyes found her in the dimness as she lay there breathing hard, her body naked, pretty brown skin against white sheets. The buzzing had stopped, and there I stood in the almost silence...looking crazy.

"Oh, shit! Sorry-sorry-sorry! I—" I spun around and left the room, embarrassed as hell and kind of turned on. Actually, I was *extremely* turned on. Something about the smell of pussy...

I rushed to my room, closing the door behind me and leaning against it as I looked down my body where my dick was tenting my pants.

Shit.

I'm unsure how long I stood there fighting the urge to head back to her room and ask for some pussy before I finally crawled into my bed and took care of my hard dick myself.

NURI

I wanted to disappear, evaporate, metamorphose into a whole new person, anything other than face Maleek Jones, my very kind boss, after he caught me in the middle of damn near cauterizing my clit with that rose toy.

Shit, shit, shit!

Motherfucking fuck!

And yet another shit!

It was my damn mouth. That rose thing made me scream. I'd discovered that the first time I used it and somehow managed not to wake the whole house up. That was why I opted to use it in the middle of the day, when I thought no one would be home. That's what I got for being greedy. I'd experienced an orgasm so great earlier in the day that I decided to go for round two and miscalculated the time or lost track of it or something! Now, I wasn't sure how I would ever face the man again.

Luckily, I didn't run into him when I left to pick up the kids or when we returned to the house. He had a home game that night but decided the kids shouldn't attend it. We'd both agreed that attending games on school nights wasn't a good idea. All I could do was hope he'd decide to slip out the house when he left for the game, but I knew that wasn't going to happen. He never left without letting the kids know.

And of course, I was right.

The kids were at the kitchen table eating their after-school snacks and I was in the pantry grabbing some stuff to make dinner when I heard his voice. I froze, standing in the middle of the spacious pantry holding a bag of rice like a deer in headlights, silently praying that he'd just leave without speaking to me.

Then I heard him ask, "Where's Nuri?" and groaned inwardly.

"In the kitchen," Junior informed him.

I thought about trying to quietly close the pantry door but decided not to take it that far.

"Hey," came his voice, silky and deep and...uncertain.

Lifting my eyes, I looked into his and almost whispered, "Hey."

He let his eyes drag over my body before fixing them on my face again. I did the same to him. I loved seeing him in a suit and tie on game days. He always looked extra fine.

Licking his very nice, thick lips, he said, "I'm heading out. Y'all are gonna watch the game on TV, right?"

"Yes," I confirmed with a nod.

"Cool. See you later."

"Okay."

I held my breath as we stood there staring at each other before he began, "Nuri—"

I shook my head. "Please don't. I can't..."

Stepping into the pantry, he closed the door behind him, moving so close to me that I not only released my breath, I gasped.

"Nuri," he murmured, "You ain't got nothing to be ashamed of. I only busted in on you because I thought you were in danger."

"I can see why you thought that," I admitted. I did sound like I was being attacked. Shit, I *was* being attacked...by that rose.

"I'ma get your door fixed."

"Okay."

"You got a man, Nuri?"

My eyes widened as he moved even closer to me, the scent of his soap and cologne tormenting me. "Uh...at the moment? No."

"Well..." He lowered his face so that it was even with mine, his eyes searching my face for a moment before he finally finished with, "Just know, I can help you with whatever you need help with. Including...*that*." His mouth was mere centimeters from mine as he spoke, his warm breath caressing my lips.

I blinked a few times before replying, "But...uh...you're my boss."

"This ain't got nothing to do with that. I know how to separate business from pleasure," he explained, and then he left.

MALEEK

I'd just stepped through the door and was keying the code into the alarm panel when I heard, "You're engaged."

Although its usual soft, gentle tone, Nuri's voice startled me, causing me to spin around and search for her in the near darkness of the foyer. There she sat on the stairs, about five steps from the bottom.

"It's late. What are you doing up?" I asked.

"Can't sleep."

"Why? Something wrong?"

"Yes. You made me a proposition earlier, but you're engaged."

"Not anymore. We're not together, remember?"

"So, you're on the rebound. I don't want to be rebound pussy. Not even for you."

Duffel bag in hand, I walked over to the stairs. "Who said that's all you'd be?"

"You're on the rebound, aren't you? Weren't you and Tasha together for years?"

"You been researching me?" I queried, placing the bag on the floor and my foot on the bottom step.

"You're my employer. Of course, I have."

"And what did you learn?" I was on the second step now.

"A lot."

"A lot good or a lot bad?"

"Good."

"That's nice to hear," I said as I stood right in front of her. "So...
you can't sleep because I want to have sex with you?"

"No. I can't sleep because I want you to have sex with me. *Bad*."

I closed my eyes and willed my dick not to get excited. As tired as
I was, the attempted willing still didn't work. Just that quickly, my
shit was on brick. "You do?"

"Yeah, you're the reason I was...doing what I was doing when you
caught me. I...thought no one would be home. Otherwise, I wouldn't
have done it."

"I'm glad you did."

I heard her gasp, which made me smile.

"Nuri—"

"I don't want things to get weird. I also don't want to get fired,
but I do want to...you know."

"You won't get fired, and I won't let things get weird."

"Even after you and Tasha get back together?"

"I...I don't want to be with Tasha. I haven't wanted to be with her
in a long time, so that ain't happening."

Silence from Nuri, so I bent over, bringing my face close to hers,
the familiar scent of vanilla and oranges filling my nose. "Can I kiss
you?"

"Uh...yes," she breathed.

So, I did. I pressed my lips to hers, and afterwards, said, "Just
think about it, and when you're ready, all you gotta do is tell me."

"Okay," she whispered.

18

NURI

"Girlllll, this is so nice! Like, damn!" Coco gushed as I led her from the foyer into the kitchen.

"Yeah, it's a beautiful house," I agreed.

"You got your own room and everything?"

"Yep."

"Big improvement from my couch, huh?" she asked as she plopped down at the table. We were having lunch together since it was her off day. "Reign was telling me how nice this place was after she came and braided your hair, but wow!"

Pulling the food she'd picked up from *Sharks* out of its bag, I asked, "Did she do your hair? I like the white with the purple."

"Yup. You know she kills the knotless braids."

"True."

"So...I know the kids are at school, but where's your boss?"

"Probably up in his room."

"Oh."

Looking up from my tray, I asked, "Oh, what?"

Coco shrugged. "I just thought I'd get to see him."

"What's that I smell?" Maleek bellowed. I almost leapt from my seat at hearing his voice.

"Oh, shit!" Coco screeched, obviously as startled as I was.

Maleek grinned. "My bad. I ain't mean to scare y'all."

Catching my breath, I placed a hand to my chest. "Well, you scared me to death!"

"You must not be living right," he jibed. "Who we got here?" he asked, nodding toward Coco.

"Hey! I'm Coco, Nuri's bestie!" she piped.

"Uh, yeah. This is Coco Bassey. Coco, this is my boss, Maleek Jones," I said.

"Oh, you're the one who goes to my games with Nuri sometimes," Maleek said, smiling down at my friend.

"Yes! Those games are crazy! I really enjoy them," Coco replied.

"Good, good. Um, can I speak to you for a minute, Nuri?" Maleek requested.

I stared at him for a moment before nodding. "Sure."

Following him out of the kitchen and into the formal dining room that we rarely used, I felt a sense of dread come over me. Was he about to fire my ass or something?

Once in the dining room, he advanced to the window, moving the white day curtain as he peered outside. "It's been a few days."

"A few days?" I repeated, my brow creased as I stood just inside the room.

"Since we talked about us having sex."

Oh. "Uh..."

"Have you been thinking about it?"

"Constantly."

Turning to face me, he smiled as he said, "Me too. You know why I keep thinking about it?"

I shook my head.

"It's because I smelled you that day, in your bedroom."

"You smelled me?"

"Yeah, I smelled your pussy. Can't get that scent out of my nose. You smelled so good."

I swallowed. "Ummmm, thank you?"

"You're welcome. Can I fuck you? Please?"

"N-now?"

"No, after your friend leaves."

"Today? I don't think I'm ready to do it today."

"Tonight?"

"I might...what if I get loud and wake the kids up?"

"Good point. Tomorrow?"

"Yes."

"Can't wait."

"Your room or mine?"

"Where would you be more comfortable?"

"Mine, since I have that fresh new door now."

Through a chuckle, he confirmed, "Yours it is, then."

MALEEK

I miss you.

I stared at Tasha's latest text message, the most recent addition to her daily offerings of apologies and confessions. As usual, I didn't reply because I didn't know what to say. Any response from me that wasn't a lie would hurt her feelings since I didn't miss her and wasn't sure if I ever would. She still hadn't come for the rest of her things, and I figured that was by design. She was leaving the door open, trying to maintain a connection to me.

Sighing, I checked the time on my phone—1:00AM. I was having a hard time falling asleep, my mind on what I had to look forward to later that day. Nuri. Nuri with the ample curves and soft voice. Nuri with the soft lips and smooth brown skin.

Lawd have mercy.

I'd never wanted to fuck a woman so bad in my whole life!

Hopping out of bed, I left my room, heading downstairs to the kitchen, hoping to snack the damn lust out of me, and who did I run into wearing a short pink robe, her little feet in pink slippers, toenails painted white? Nuri, that's who.

She was so damn fine!

I stopped just short of touching her, my heart bouncing in my chest as I said, "Hey, can't sleep?"

"I was thirsty," she replied, holding up a glass of water I hadn't noticed.

"Yeah, so am I. Hungry, too."

"Maleek, can I ask you something?"

Leaning against the counter as she did the same against the refrigerator, I nodded. "Sure."

"When Tasha was here the last time and y'all were arguing, I couldn't help hearing y'all, and...were you really a virgin when you got with her?"

I smiled. "Yeah, why?"

"Because...does that mean you've only been with her sexually?"

I lost the smile, understanding where she was going with this line of questioning. "Yes, but that doesn't mean I'm getting back with her. I don't know how to explain what we had other than it was comfortable for me. I should've...I should've ended it long ago. I didn't out of loyalty."

"And love?"

"Not the kind of love you're thinking about."

Nuri frowned, dropping her eyes for a moment before focusing on my face again. "What does that mean? What kind of love did—do you have for her?"

"It's—I guess I love her like you'd love a friend."

"But you had sex with her?"

"Yeah."

"I don't understand."

"Sex doesn't always equal love, Nuri."

"Yeah. So...what am I to you? Another friend?"

Moving closer to her, I shook my head. "You're a woman I am

extremely attracted to who I hope to become much more than friends with."

Gazing up at me, she murmured. "Okay."

Leaning in, I kissed her, holding her face in my hands. Then I asked her, "We still on for tomorrow? Or did you change your mind?"

"We're still on for tomorrow," she confirmed.

———

I was nervous, like nervouser than a motherfucker. I mean, I was still excited about being with Nuri, touching her, feeling her, but our conversation last night reminded me that I'd only ever been with Tasha sexually. Everything I knew about pleasing a woman, I'd learned from and with her. What if I couldn't please Nuri? What if she was more experienced than me like Tasha was and I disappointed her? What if—shit!

I was so damn wound up; I couldn't really concentrate during practice—watching the clock, anticipating getting the fuck out of there so I could go home and do everything I could to outshine that toy I caught her using. I was supposed to be doing passing drills, but I kept wondering what Nuri's bountiful-ass titties were going to taste like.

"Jones! The fuck is you doing?!" Rapp yelled.

Shaking myself out of my thoughts, I realized he'd sent the puck my way without me noticing it. "My bad," I mumbled.

"Get your head right, man," he advised.

In return, I nodded and did my best to stay focused, knowing she'd be waiting for me when I got home.

19

NURI

I was so pent up, anticipation and anxiety nearly making me feel nauseous. What I was about to do, what *we* were about to do, could turn out to be the best thing that ever happened to me or the worse thing—a good decision or a horrible one—and the only way to know for sure was to do it. Lord knows I wanted to do it. I really, honestly, truly wanted to do it. Hell, at that point, I *needed* to do it before I sprained, dislocated, or fractured my whole, entire pussy from *not* doing it. What else could I do? Being in the same zip code as a man so damn chocolatey and bearded and tall would be torture enough, let alone the same house! Maleek had hooded, almond-shaped eyes in the deepest shade of brown, and his lips? Thick, and a perfect fit for mine. Big hands, big feet, fine body, and the nicest smile in the contiguous United States. A girl could easily fall in love...or lust with him; my body chose the latter.

Above all that, his kindness was what drew me to him, his kindness, his patience with the kids, his willingness to take care of them when he barely knew them, all of which displayed the condition of his heart. Maleek was a good man, a good man I hoped wasn't the type to hit it and quit it, since men were known to change on a dime. Like my granny always used to say, "You can trust a man until you can't."

She also said, "Don't get your honey where you get your money," but did I listen?

Hell no.

Why was I sitting on the foot of my bed in my favorite *Nick and Dame* t-shirt waiting to be fucked by my employer while thinking about my grandmother?

Ew.

Falling onto my back, I willed myself not to check the time again. He had practice. When he made it home, he'd be tired. I couldn't expect him to walk through the door, run in my room, and hop between my legs. Damn, was I really that much in lust with the man?

Hell yeah, a voice in my head sassed. *You're beyond that horny, sis.*

Clamping my eyes *and* thighs shut, I sighed, thinking that maybe I should've taken the edge off with RoseShawn—yes, I named him—or WandDré, but I didn't want to be in a damn coma when he arrived. Those electronically induced orgasms could knock a bitch out!

When a soft knock sounded at my door, I bolted upright and stared at it, my heart parkouring wildly as I cleared my throat and said, "Come in!"

The door eased open and there he was—as handsome as ever, no shirt with a white towel wrapped around his waist, a beautiful contrast to his dark brown skin. His grin was lopsided and instant as he said, "Hey."

Clasping my hands together in my lap, I replied, "Hey. Fresh out the shower?"

"Yeah, couldn't come in here smelling like the rink."

"Did you wash your booty hole? I heard you men have an issue with that."

Now, he was smiling widely, his words coming out on a chuckle. "What? What did you just ask me?"

"Did you wash your ass, like *literally* wash your ass?" I wasn't smiling. I was deadass serious. "With soap *and* water," I added

He, however, was bent over howling. When he got himself together, he said, "Yes, ma'am. I washed my ass. Spread my cheeks, lathered everything up. I'm good, Miss Knox."

"Great. Glad to hear it. Condom?"

He lifted his right hand, showcasing an entire damn collection of condoms.

Nodding, I stated, "Wonderful."

"Anything else? I brushed my teeth and cleaned behind my ears, too," he advised me.

"I appreciate that," I said.

"Yo, you're funny...funny *and* fine. I hope that's not a lethal combination."

"I guess you'll see in a minute."

"I guess I will."

MALEEK

When I entered the room and saw her sitting there in that big t-shirt, her eyes wide, her lips slightly parted, I almost shot off right then. Nuri was...I don't know. She was something past pretty and on the other side of beautiful. Those eyes, that pouty mouth, that smooth russet skin, that thick-as-country-cornbread-cooked-in-a-cast-iron-skillet body, those titties? Got Damn! Evidently, I had a type. I didn't even realize that until I laid eyes on Nuri because my type was one woman—*her*. She made me feel things I'd never felt before. She made me want to experiment with and explore her body like my name was Matthew Henson, and when I was done, I instinctively knew I'd want to embark on endless recon missions. I could feel it in my spirit that her pussy was just that good.

After she finished her hygiene debriefing and my mirth had

subsided, I asked, "Can I come sit next to you?" from my position just inside the room.

"I hope you came to do more than sit."

That did it. That's when I'm sure I lost my mind. It was the fact that she wasn't even *trying* to be sexy. She just *was*. Everything she did, every expression on her face, every word out of her mouth turned me on, and I was certain it wasn't just because Tasha was gone. It wasn't because it'd been a minute since I had sex, either. It was Nuri. It was simply *her*. Somehow, she'd resurrected me from an existence of sleepwalking through life.

So, the next thing I knew, I was crowding her body, bending over, cupping her face in my hands, kissing her softly, licking her lips, moaning when she opened her mouth for me. She tasted like mint—toothpaste—cool and airy, while at the same time, warm. We kissed and smacked and moaned, her hands covering mine. When we parted, her breathing was harsh, her pupils dilated in the sunlight streaming through the sheer curtains.

"Do you...do you want to close the curtains? You like it dark?" she panted.

I shook my head, rubbing my thumb over her bottom lip. So damn perfect. "No, I wanna see everything."

"Okay," she said through a hitched breath.

"You nervous, Nuri?" I asked.

She gave me a hesitant nod.

"So am I," I admitted.

With a frown, she questioned, "Why would you be nervous?"

My eyes surveyed her face before I spoke. "It's like...like when I skate out on the ice before a game. I'm always so pumped up. I know I've done it a million times. I know the game like I know the back of my hand. I've trained. I've practiced, but for me, every game feels like my first game. I...it's as if I erase the past every time. This, *you*...you feel like my first time, Nuri, and I'm scared I'll disappoint you."

She moved her head a few inches so that her lips met mine in a kiss so sweet; it made me whimper. "You won't disappoint me. You *can't* disappoint me," she softly said.

I lost my fucking mind *again*, time jumped, and when full awareness returned to me, I was in the bed with her, my tongue exploring her mouth, my hands squeezing her breasts. The towel was gone and so was her shirt. Our bodies were pressed together, my erection pinned between us. I felt frenetic inside, overcome with an urgency so strong that I felt unbalanced as I devoured her mouth.

My need for oxygen forced me to break our connection, and I reluctantly left the bed and her body, staring down at her while trying to calm myself. My damn hands were shaking. My dick was leaking and shit. I didn't know I could want *anything* this badly.

"What?" she squeaked, her eyebrows in a tangle. "You don't...did you change your mind?"

I quickly shook my head. "No. I just...I want you so fucking bad. I'm tryna take it slow but—"

Her eyes fell to my dick, rock hard and *too* damn ready. "Let's just do it. Just fuck me. *Please.*"

Gooooot damn! Was she *trying* to make me bust on contact?

"Uh...okay. Okay." I bent over, grabbing one of the handful of condoms that somehow ended up on the floor, opened the wrapper, and covered myself. Then I was back in the bed, between her thighs. With my dick resting on her pussy, I could feel heat radiating from inside her.

My God.

I rubbed her clit with my fingertip, making her flinch and cry out before sliding a finger inside her. "So fucking tight!" I groaned.

"Oh!" she whined.

I fingered her for as long as I could stand not being inside her, and then I lined my dick up with the gateway to her heaven, tried to ease inside but couldn't. So, I tried again, and again... *and again* before it hit me. I gazed down at her face to see that her eyes were squeezed shut, her brow deeply furrowed, and I could tell she was holding her breath. Was she...? Nah, it couldn't be. Still, I had to ask.

"Are you...are you a virgin, Nuri?"

Her eyes popped open and almost instantly began to fill with tears as she whimpered, "Yes."

20

NURI

I watched as shock registered on his face. I was hoping I wouldn't have to admit it, that we'd just do it. I wasn't expecting him to be so big, though.

Big with a capital B. I. G.

"Why didn't you tell me?" he asked, his body hovering over mine. He was still between my legs, and I *still* wanted him to fuck me.

"I don't know. Didn't think it mattered," I lied.

"Didn't think it mattered? It *does*, it...you sure you want to do this with me? You want to lose your virginity with *me*? Why?"

"Because you're the only man I've ever known who deserves it."

His eyes ballooned as he licked his lips.

"You don't wanna do it now?" I asked. "I'll understand if you don't."

"Naw, that ain't it. I just...this is special, Nuri. More so than I thought."

"I know."

"And I ain't got no little dick."

"I see that. I feel it, too."

"I'll take it easy and go slow."

I nodded, closing my eyes as he kissed me, his hand finding my clit and making me want to scoot up the bed. We kissed as he stroked me, causing pressure to build and my breathing to stutter. Then a finger was inside me as he kept rubbing my clit. He fingered and rubbed and stroked me until I tore my mouth from his, throwing my head back while trying to remember how to breathe. As I recovered from the orgasm, I felt him try to breach me again, but this time, he didn't stop, and as he inched his way inside me, I gasped, grabbing his shoulders to anchor myself. I wasn't expecting it to feel so uncomfortable...so painful.

What felt like ages passed before I heard him say, "Open your eyes, Nuri, and breathe. I'm in." His voice was shaky, strained.

I peered up at him, noting the sweat on his forehead. "All the way in?"

He nodded. "Yeah, as much of me that'll fit."

"Can we make all of it fit?"

"All? I don't think so. If we lift your legs, I can probably fit more."

"Let's do that."

His eyes widened. "It's your first time. I...I don't want to hurt you."

"You're already hurting me. Go deeper," I countered.

"Okay," he said. "Shit, okay. Give me a second. I gotta calm the fuck down."

More than a second later, I lifted my legs, placing them on his shoulders. Almost instantly, he slipped deeper inside me, making me gasp.

"Oh, my damn! Shit!" he grunted. "Fuck, Nuri! H-how do you feel?"

"Full, and it...it still hurts."

"I know. I'm sorry. Want me to—"

"I want you to fuck me, Maleek. That's what I want."

He nodded again, easing back and groaning, "I'ont wanna bust yet, but you so damn tight!"

I clutched his arms as he rocked in and out of me, slowly at first. Then he picked up speed, setting a pace and rhythm that soon added pleasure to the ever-present pain. He was rubbing against a spot inside of me that made my belly quiver and slowly chipped away my sanity. He rubbed my clit while he fucked me, causing me to whimper his name as pressure began to pool inside my core again. I could hear him, his moans, my name coming breathlessly from his lips every time he dove deeper inside me. I felt tears escaping my eyes as the pressure inside me summited, my mouth dropping open as ecstasy poured over me, blocking all sound and making me feel like I was somewhere outside my body looking in.

In an instant, I was back and Maleek was yelling, "Shit! Shit! Shii-iiiit!" as his dick pulsed inside me.

I lay there, chest heaving, heart beating erratically as his body twitched. His lips were on my neck, my cheeks, my mouth. "Thank you. Nuri. Thank you," he whispered. "Thank you, baby."

21

MALEEK

We were still in her bed, me spooned behind her fighting not to squeeze her titties, my dick seemingly permanently hard, my mind in a post-pussy fog. I was feeling tingly and giddy, and I had no idea why. Was it her pussy, the fact that she'd chosen me to be her first? Or was it just her?

Again, it was her.

Nuri was special. I saw that from day one, so special that I was lying behind her with a big, stupid-ass grin on my face.

"You okay?" I asked into her shoulder as I kissed it.

"Yeah, I think so. Was it...did you like it? The sex, I mean?" she answered.

The first words in my mind were *hell motherfucking yes!* Instead, I said, "I *loved* it. Did you? Was it worth the wait? Glad you chose me?"

"Yes. It hurt, but...I don't know. I liked it."

"Good. It'll get better, easier."

"Yeah."

"Uh, Nuri...why were you still a virgin?"

"Because I was taught not to give my body to men who don't deserve it. Like I said, you're the only man I've ever known who deserves it."

"But how can you know that when you barely know me?"

"I know enough. I know you have a good heart. I know I feel safe with you."

Her words made my heart thud and my eyes mist. *She feels safe with me.* "You had any boyfriends?"

"Yes, and we kissed, touched, but no penetration. No oral, either."

"Well, I'm honored. I...Nuri?"

"Yes?"

"I ain't trying to be greedy, and I know you're sore, but my dick is hard again and, um..."

"I wanna do it again."

Shit!

"Okay, but I need to do something first," I said.

"Something like what?" she inquired.

I moved, rolling her on her back and lowering myself until my head was between her thighs. When I opened her labia and licked her clit, she gasped, her thighs closing a little, but I kept licking, slow and easy, taking my time tasting her and committing her flavor to memory. My ears were filled with her soft pants and moans and whimpers as she wiggled beneath me. She was so gone that she started babbling as I clutched her soft thighs and feasted on her. I ate her pussy like I was making up for lost time, and when she began screaming my name, I didn't let up. I *couldn't* let up. I didn't take my mouth off her until I felt her hands pushing my head and heard her beg, "I can't. I...*please.*"

I left the dinner table, my beard wet as I came face to face with her, seeing the tears staining her cheeks. "How do you feel?" I asked.

In response, she grabbed my face, pulling it to hers in a frantic, chaotic kiss that I eagerly returned. We shared her flavor for long minutes before I broke the connection.

"No," she whined.

"Condom," I explained.

She gave me a nod, and I reluctantly left the bed and her sinful body, quickly sheathing myself and rejoining her. I kissed her, lowered my head to suck her juicy-ass titties, and when I lifted my head again, I asked, "You ready?"

She quickly nodded, so I eased inside her.

"Got damn!" I yelled involuntarily. This pussy was going to drive my ass crazy. I felt that shit in my soul.

"Oh my god!" she cried. "Maleek! Maleeeeeeeek!"

I had to close my eyes and concentrate to keep from busting on initiation. Honestly, at that point, the thought of being inside her was enough for me to start shooting my shit all over the place, but I maintained, stroking her with restraint, letting pleasure coat my entire body as I gripped the sheet underneath us and stared down at her like she was a damn miracle. Maybe she was. Maybe she was something that only came along once in a lifetime. She was rare for damn sure, rare and precious.

"Nuri, open your eyes, baby. Look at me," I groaned. "Look at me, baby. I need to see those pretty eyes."

She popped them open, her lids low, her expression lazy.

"Thank you for choosing me," I grunted. "Thank you so...fucking...much."

Her eyelashes fluttered as she reached up and began tracing my lips with her soft finger. Something about that act made my mind snap once again. I thrusted harder, deeper, making her throw her head back and scream my name, and when I busted, I'm not ashamed to admit that tears were flooding my face.

When I figured out how to talk again, I asked, "You on birth control, Nuri?"

"No," she supplied.

"Can you get on some? I'm clean, but I'll get tested again if you want me to."

"I'll make an appointment."

NURI

We took a shower together, and I got a good look at him and...*it*.

Beautiful.

All of him was beautiful.

I watched him lather up as I attempted to do the same, but his naked body made it hard for me to concentrate.

"You a'ight?" he asked, his eyes on me as he dragged the washcloth over his abs.

I gave him a nod. "Yes...can I touch it?"

"My dick? Yeah. You can do whatever you want with it at this point. Give me your hand."

I proffered my hand to him, watching as he placed it around his length. He covered my hand with his as I rubbed and squeezed him, closing his eyes and dropping his head between his shoulder blades. Then he lifted his hand from mine, using it to brace himself on the shower wall.

I caressed and rubbed him. It felt smooth, the veins were spongy, and it was so damn...hard. Stunning. It was stunning. Just touching it triggered a deluge between my legs.

"I wanna watch you touch yourself," I told him.

His head dipped, his eyelids at half-mast as he licked his lips. His, "Okay," was thick, strangled.

The shower was huge with dual heads, and as the one pointed toward me battered my body with steamy water, I observed him gliding his big hand up and down his dick, his eyes glued to me. He stroked and stroked and stroked, his breathing growing labored, grunts spilling from his mouth. Through it all, he never broke eye contact with me. I observed as his breathing grew uneven and his moans lifted in volume until he exploded all over the place, including me. His warm stickiness splattered my stomach, and I didn't care. I was too amazed, too turned on, too mesmerized to care. Reaching down, I wiped his cum from my skin, and with my eyes stapled to his dick, I reached for it, rubbing his cream all over it. Almost instantly, it sprung to life again.

"Shit," he breathed. "*Fuck*. Nuri, you're gonna kill me."

I moved closer to him. "I wanna cum, too," I said, gazing up at him.

"Baby, you're already sore," he whispered.

"Use your hand," I replied.

In a second, his fingers were between my thighs, between my folds, and then inside me. His other hand held my face as we kissed hungrily. I felt wired as he worked to give me what I'd asked for, and it didn't take long for him to achieve that goal given my already heightened state of arousal. When an orgasm began to overwhelm me, I clutched his shoulders and screamed his name into his mouth.

———

After D-Day, AKA the day Maleek Jones dropped that bomb-ass dick on me, I don't think there was a second we were in a room together where he wasn't staring at me all while I fought not to stare at him. Of course, I failed. That was how I knew his eyes were on me. When our gazes met, he'd smile at me. I'd smile back, and sometimes, we'd start laughing. It all felt so good, euphoric.

We did it twice that first day—I wasn't sure if the shower encounter counted as round three—and then I had to pick the kids up from school. He didn't have a game that night, so he chilled with me and the kids. We had pizza delivered because I was too post-dick exhausted to cook. Then we both helped the kids with their homework. Getting them ready for bed was a collaborative effort as well. After that, we went our separate ways—him to his room and me to mine.

It was late and I was half asleep when I heard a soft knock at my door, followed by a muted baritone voice whispering my name. The door opened before I could respond, revealing a gorgeous shadow of a physique.

"Can I come in?" he asked.

"Yes," I replied.

"Can I have some more pussy?"

"You sure can."

He closed my door, and in a flash, he was in my bed, his mouth on mine, then on my neck, my breasts, my...pussy. As he devoured me, I felt, I don't know, wild? Maybe a little insane? Like I was losing my whole-ass mind? My heart raced, my legs shook, and my hands were moving on their own accord, eventually clutching his head. I wanted him to stop but I needed him to keep going because I was almost there. I could feel it coming and coming and—

I clamped a hand over my mouth, sounding like a muffled feral animal as the bubble inside me popped, sending waves of electricity to every single crevice of my body. Now, he was kissing me sloppily, urgently, while he slid inside me, throwing his head back as I sucked in a breath. This man was going to fuck me to death...and I was going to let him.

"Maleek, oh god," I cried softly.

I would've said more had he not recaptured my mouth, one big hand gripping my left breast, the other bearing the weight of his body. I was sore, so sore, and full and wet, all of that somehow working together to make tears pool in my eyes and butterflies swarm my belly. Every part of my body was sensitive and frayed. It was so pleasurably odd that if someone had tried to explain these sensations to me, I wouldn't have understood. I *still* didn't understand, but I knew I wanted to do it again...and again...and again.

Amen.

"You look different. You been working out or something. You got this glowing, dewy look on your face," Coco rambled as we walked. I needed to shop for groceries, and she'd asked to tag along.

"I guess you can call it working out," I replied, stopping to grab a couple packages of spaghetti pasta since the kids loved my spaghetti.

"You guess—bitch, wait! Have you been..." She lowered her voice before continuing, "Have you been having sex? You finally let go of that virginity you've been holding on to for dear life?"

"I'm selective. You know that."

"Ho', answer the question!"

I sighed, continuing down the aisle while pushing the half-full buggy. "I can confirm that I am no longer a virgin."

"What?!" she shrieked. "Who?!"

Nothing from me.

"Wait-wait-wait! Your boss? I knew it! I *knew* he liked you!"

"How'd you know that?" I asked, stopping to look at her.

"The way he looks at you, like you're a juicy steak and a diamond rolled into one."

"Oh."

She grabbed me, pulling me into a tight hug, and since she was taller than me, I ended up being half smothered by her titties. "I'm so happy for you! I *know* he got good dick. Good choice, sis. Good choice!"

Once she released me and I caught my breath, I said, "Isn't he?"

Him: *Hey*

Frowning, I returned his text with: *Hey?*

Him: *Why the question mark?*

Me: *Because we're in the same room. I'm looking right at you.*

Him: *Yeah, but the kids are sitting between us and they don't need to hear what I gotta tell you.*

We were in the living room watching *Encanto* for the one-trillionth time. It was Jules' night to pick our movie. Junior was *not* happy.

Me: *And what is it that you just gotta say?*

Him: *I can still taste your pussy from last night. Fucking scrumptious.*

I looked up to see him grinning at me.

Me: *I hate you.*

We locked eyes and both started laughing.

"Why y'all laughing? This part ain't even funny. I hate this movie!" Junior fussed.

Maleek: *I can't wait to eat you again and I ain't leaving not one crumb on the table.*

One thing about Maleek Jones, he might've told me a joke, but he never told me a lie. He ate my coochie until I damn near passed out that night.

22

MALEEK

"Jules, Junior, we're going to talk today," Dr. Rice informed them.

"About what?" Junior asked. He, Jules, and Dr. Rice all sat on these big cushions on the floor of her office.

"Whatever you guys want to talk about," Dr. Rice explained. "Maleek is going to step out this time, so it'll just be the three of us."

I stood from my seat. "Yeah, I'll be right outside in the lobby where Miss Nuri is."

I was heading toward the door when I heard a shrill, tiny, "No!" Then I felt a small hand grab mine. I looked down to see it was Jules sharing one of her words for the first time in weeks, her face upturned, her little eyes, the ones she shared with me and Junior, pleading with me.

I squatted beside her, taking both her hands. "Hey, I'll be right outside. I promise."

Shaking her head, she said, "No-no-no-no!"

So, I said, "Okay, I'll stay," reclaiming my seat with her glued to my side. She even refused to sit on the floor until Dr. Rice got me a cushion so I could sit down there with them. Once we were all settled, Junior started giving us NHL stats, really impressive stuff. It was stuff I knew but still interesting.

"...and did you know there was a Black hockey league that started in Canada in 1895? That's like ancient times!" Junior gushed.

"I didn't know that," Dr. Rice said. "Junior, you sure know a lot about hockey. Where'd you learn all of this information?"

"From my dad. He talked about hockey all the time because of Maleek. He always said Maleek was the best in the league. He liked talking to me about it because I'm a boy, but he'd tell Jules stuff, too," Junior replied.

"I see. Jules, what did your father tell you?" Dr. Rice questioned.

Jules, who was basically sitting under me, her tiny hand in mine, looked up at me. In turn, I smiled at her.

With her eyes still on me, she softly said, "He told me that after that guy from the Blackhawks tripped you that time, you should've beat his ass."

I tried not to, but I ended up laughing before I said, "Really?"

Jules smiled as she nodded.

I rubbed the top of her head and turned my attention to Junior as he spouted off more hockey facts.

NURI

Nine words.

It only took nine words.

Maleek and I were discussing Thanksgiving, which I, of course, was spending with him and the kids plus his mother, when I made my first mistake. I told him I'd been on the pill for eight days, meaning our freaky free-for-all could commence. Then came the nine words: *"I want you to fuck me from the back."*

His response? "Say less."

The next thing I knew, I was bent over the kitchen counter *bucket nekkid* in the middle of a bright Tuesday morning getting fucked like there was no tomorrow. I couldn't stop moaning, a sound that coupled well with the rhythm of Maleek's balls smacking my ass and his repeated grunts of, "This some good fucking pussy!"

Not gonna lie, I was in Maleek Jones heaven.

MALEEK

"Got damn, Jones! You been *sprinting* up out of here after practice lately! Act like your woman ain't left you!" Ford said as I hurriedly dressed in the locker room.

"What you mean?" was how I chose to respond. "I'm just ready to go home."

He didn't reply, so I looked up to see him staring at me with this crazy expression on his face.

"Nigga, what?!" I growled.

"You motherfucker! You got another woman! That's why you been all perky and shit lately," he said.

"I'm a got damn man. I ain't *never* been perky," I shot back.

"Pussy good, too, ain't it? I can tell, and you been eating it. Your beard all luxurious and shit."

Ford was a fucking fool. An intuitive fool, but a fool, nonetheless. So I said, "Fuck you, Ford."

"And you got that pussy anticipation look in your eyes, like it's some guaranteed ass in your near future. You must be headed to her place 'cause the nanny living with y'all now, ain't she?"

Nothing from me.

"Jones! You fucking the nanny?!"

"He is?!" That was Rapp, coming out of nowhere.

I didn't say a word as I tied the laces on my Jordans.

"When we gon' meet this nanny with the yellow brick pussy?" That was Ford's dumb ass again.

I *had* to say something at that point. "The *what* pussy?"

"Yellow brick, ease on down the road, mean ole lion pussy," Ford

reiterated, "because your ass is in the Land of Oz. You are gone! Shiiiiid, I ain't never seen you this frisky before."

"First perky and now frisky? Number your days, Ford."

"What?" he said, dragging the word out. "I'm just saying, you
been acting real spunky here lately."

"I mean...he ain't lying," Rapp agreed. "You been mad peppy, my
guy."

"You know what?" I said, "Fuck both of y'all." Grinning, I
grabbed my duffel bag and left.

We were kissing—one of my favorite things to do with Nuri—as I
rubbed my hands up and down her back. It was the middle of the
day and I'd found her in the laundry room folding clothes. Her
mouth felt and tasted so good. Hell, her *everything* felt and tasted
good. I'd never eaten ass before, but I'd mentally added eating Nuri's
ass to my to-do list because I was willing to wager my entire salary
that it tasted good, too.

Leaving her mouth, I licked her neck and murmured, "I could
fucking kiss and lick on you all day and all night."

"You basically already do," she said, her hand clutching the back
of my head.

I chuckled, stood up straight, held her around her waist, and
lifted her up, sitting her on the washer and making her yelp. When I
started tugging at the jogging pants she had on, she lifted her ass for
me. Once the bottom half of her was naked, I pulled her to the edge
of the washer, spread those immaculate thighs of hers, and kissed
my way from her right knee to her plump pussy. Her hands hit the
top of the washer as she leaned back and moaned. I reached up,
gently squeezing her belly meat as I licked and slurped all over her
pussy, a pussy that stayed on my mind. I had no idea life could be
like this. So good, so right. I owed Tasha an apology. I should've freed
her long ago because I never felt for her in seven years what I almost
instantly felt for Nuri Knox. I was a fucking addict when it came to

this woman and every curve she was blessed with. But honestly, this was more than physical, much more. Nuri was a nurturer, a caregiver with a pure heart. She was a light, and evidently, I was strongly attracted to all of that. I honestly didn't realize that before her. I didn't know I could feel, *really feel*, until her.

I added my fingers to the mix, sliding them inside her wet, tight, steaming hot treasure while sucking on her clit. Her breathing was loud, her hands were now gripping my ears, and only a few moments passed before the sound of her labored breathing ceased, her body went rigid, and she shrieked my name.

I took my mouth from her, sliding my fingers out her pussy and licking them as I stood, using my free hand to pull my pants down. My dick sprang free as I leaned in to kiss her, grabbing her legs and placing them on my shoulders. Then I was inside her, raw, no barrier, her slick heat making me close my eyes and sigh.

"Nuri...Nuri, you're so fucking good!" I whined. "Shit, baby. Why you feel so good?"

I slid in and out of her, my whole body feeling like it was about to bust. Nuri was the eighth world wonder, an inexplicable phenomenon. An unsolved mystery. *My* unsolved mystery. My addiction. My *one*.

As she screamed her way through another orgasm, I felt my nut coming and braced myself. While emptying inside her, there was only one thought in my mind—*my pussy.*

23

NURI

We sat at the kitchen table, Maleek in his new regular seat beside me with his hand squeezing my thigh. We played it cool around the kids, neither of us wanting to confuse them when we hadn't even defined what it was we were doing other than enjoying each other. It was like Maleek couldn't help himself, though. He *had* to touch me, and shit, I wasn't complaining. But pretending we were still merely employer and employee was taxing. We'd long abandoned our agreement to only have sex while the kids were at school, and I swore we were going to fuck around and smother ourselves trying to keep from yelling. Right now, his hand on me had my clit doing that Beyoncé *Cuff It* dance. At this rate, he was going to be eating my pussy on the Thanksgiving table for all to see. The sad part? I would let it happen. Now, I understood why Tasha had acted such a fool. Maleek had *Magical School Bus* dick!

. . .

The kids were having some TV time before bed, and I was bent over, loading the dishwasher when I felt him behind me. Like right behind me, his dick poking me in the ass.

Standing erect, I said, "You need help. You're a damn nympho."

Kissing the side of my neck, he slid his arms around my waist and said into my ear, "Only for you, Miss Knox."

"You had me wet at dinner."

"Shit!"

"And if you keep on, the kids are gonna find out we're..."

"We're what?" he asked, kissing the other side of my neck.

"I don't know. What exactly *are* we doing?"

"Whatever you wanna do, whenever you wanna do it. I swear, I'd follow you into a pit of fire."

"You would?"

"Hell yeah."

I spun around, looking him in the eye. "It feels weird that you still pay me with all the...personal stuff we've been doing."

"I'm paying you for taking care of the kids, not for your pussy. You know that."

"I do. It just...I don't know. It makes me uncomfortable."

"Okay. I'ma have to fire you, then, because we can't stop fucking. I will literally cry if we stop doing that."

With a roll of my eyes, I expressed, "Maleek, I'm serious."

"Shiiiiid, so am I!"

I sighed.

"A'ight, listen," he said, cradling my face in his hands, "look at it as me providing for my woman."

"Your...woman?"

"My one and only...if that's okay with you, Miss Knox."

Wearing a smile so wide my cheeks ached, I replied, "That's more than okay with me, Mr. Jones."

MALEEK

"Maleek, this is Kita, Tasha's mother. Of course, you probably recognize my voice, but this is a new number. I'm sure you don't have it programmed in your phone. I'm calling to see what can be done to fix things between you and my baby. She's miserable without you, and I'm sure you feel the same without her. My poor baby broke down when you canceled her credit cards and had her things delivered to my house instead of bringing them yourself, and she says you've been ignoring her texts and calls. Surely, those kids can't mean more to you than the seven years you spent with Tasha. Please call me back, honey."

I deleted the voicemail from Tasha's mom and sighed as I lay in my bed. It was just after midnight, and I was trying to give Nuri a break from fucking. We'd been at it nonstop, with me initiating every time because I just couldn't help myself. Everything in this relationship with Nuri was so different. Tasha had always initiated sex, she'd always planned just about everything in our lives, and I thought I liked that. Maybe I did. Maybe the person I was with her needed her to take the lead. Hell, on the real, I was still growing, learning, and trying to figure things out, including things about myself, for the better part of that relationship. I wasn't sure what I wanted other than a career playing hockey. Now I knew for sure that I wanted to take care of my siblings and I wanted to be with Nuri...forever.

A soft knock at my door pulled me from my thoughts, and certain that it was one of the kids, I said, "Come in!"

When I saw that it was Nuri in her little pink robe and pink slippers, I seriously started salivating.

"Hey," I said with a grin.

She smiled. "Hey."

Then we just stared at each other like a couple lovesick puppies until I asked, "You missed me?"

She nodded. "Yeah. I was waiting for you."

"Thought I'd give you a break."

"I don't remember asking for one."

Shit!

"And there's something I wanna try. Something sexual," she added.

Got. Damn!

"So come try it then, baby," I said.

She dropped her robe, revealing her nakedness and making me moan, "You're so fucking fine, baby. Ain't another woman in this world who comes close to you."

As she climbed into the bed and under the covers with me, she said, "Thank you. Can you turn the lamp off?"

"Yeah."

As soon as the room went black, I felt her shift beside me, felt the covers slide off me, felt her hand in my boxers, felt her grab my dick, felt her slide it out the slot in the front of my underwear, and then? And then I felt her mouth on me. I gasped, grabbing the sheet underneath me with both hands. My toes started throwing up gang signs as my mouth fell open. How the fuck was it possible for her mouth to feel so good? I wasn't ready for this to be what she wanted to try, and the shock mixed with the pleasure had my nut teetering right at the edge of an explosion.

"Wait, shit...wait, Nuri. Stop, baby," I begged.

Her voice sounded so small as she asked, "Why? Am I not doing it right? I watched some videos and—"

"Naw, you doing it right. You doing it righter than a motherfucker, actually. You doing it so right that I'm about to bust already."

"Well, isn't that the goal?"

"Yeah, but—"

That mouth was on me again, forcing me to clamp a hand over mine to keep from crying out. So instead, I sounded like a broken pickup truck or some shit, my groans and grunts muffled as she sucked every stitch of my mortal soul from my body.

When I had halfway recovered and was lying in my bed with her in my arms, I said, "I want you to move into my room. I don't want to sleep without you."

"Um, what about—" Nuri began, but I cut her off.

"I'm gonna tell the kids you're my girlfriend. We've been sneaking around for a minute now. I'm tired of hiding it," I informed her.

"O...okay, but can you do something for me?"

"Anything."

"Buy a new bed."

"Consider it done."

———

Nuri: *Good game, Jones. Me and the kids lost it when you made that goal.*

Me: *Thank you. You gonna give me some celebratory pussy when I get home?*

Nuri: *Yeah. I want you to teach me how to ride you.*

My dick was hard so fast that I got a little lightheaded.

Me: *What does that song say? Save a horse ride a nigga? I'm that nigga.*

Nuri: *LMAO! It's ride a cowboy.*

Me: *Same thing. I miss you.*

Nuri: *Miss you too. I'll be waiting for you. Naked. In bed.*

Abba, father!

"Hey, what you doing? Looking at ass pics of your new woman?"

I glanced up to see Rapp dropping into the seat beside me on the bus. We were heading to the airport after our game in Dallas.

My answer was to give him my middle finger, my eyes still on my phone.

Rapp laughed, muttering, "Sensitive ass. I can't wait to meet this woman. I ain't never seen you this happy before."

I looked up at him and shrugged. "I ain't never *been* this happy before. I don't know, it's like...she fits me. Like, she was made for me, and I was made for her."

"Damn, that's deep."

"Yeah."

"Hey, can I ask you something?"

"Shoot."

"Okay, so...you know me and Indira been together for a good little minute, and we're good. I care about her, and I ain't got no plans of going anywhere, but I don't think I'm ready for marriage."

"Okay..."

"Yeah, so the thing is, she said if I don't propose to her by the end of the year, she's leaving me."

"And?"

"And...I'ma do it. A nigga ain't tryna be alone."

"You love her?"

"Huh?"

"Man, you heard me."

He sighed. "Yeah. I mean...yeah."

"A'ight, so what do you wanna ask me?"

He stared at me.

"You want me to tell you not to do it? Is that it?"

His grown, taller than me ass just shrugged.

"I ain't gon' do that, but I will say this: in my case, I stayed with Tasha more out of loyalty than love. I appreciated her for sticking with me when I honestly thought I didn't deserve anybody's love. I proposed because I wanted to make her happy. I bought a house to make her happy, too. What I should've done was let her go so she could find a man who could really love her because now I know I couldn't, and that ain't on her. It's on me. I made myself do a lot of shit to stay with Tasha that I willingly do for my woman now. When you're with the right one, you don't question shit like this, you know? I was trying not to hurt Tasha, but it would've been better to cut the cord years ago because when she finds out about me and Nuri, it's gon' kill her."

"Nuri. Nice name."

"An even nicer woman."

"Why you think she gon' be upset? Because you moved on so fast?"

"That, and *she* hired her to nanny my siblings."

"Damn."

"I know."

24

MALEEK

"Boyfriend and girlfriend?!" Junior basically yelled.

With a frown, Jules quietly added, "Like *The Princess and the Frog*?"

Did she just call me a frog?

I glanced over at Nuri, who kept her eyes on her plate as she very conspicuously tried not to laugh.

"I mean, yes...I guess," I answered.

Jules smiled. "That's nice."

Junior shrugged. "Okay. Can I play *NHL* on the Xbox? I'm all done eating."

Well, damn.

"Uh, yeah. Sure, man," I said.

"Thank you!" Junior chirped, leaving the dinner table and jetting out of the kitchen.

"Can I watch him?" Jules asked.

I was so happy she was talking more that I *couldn't* refuse her. "Yep."

"Well, that went well," Nuri said once we were alone.

"Yeah, they basically don't give a shit," I observed.

"At all."

I shook my head. "All that damn sneaking around for nothing."

"Right, but I don't know why I'm surprised. They love you, Maleek. In their eyes, you can do no wrong."

"I see!"

I was sitting there thinking about how therapy was helping Jules—it was slow going, but it was definitely helping her—when I heard Nuri's chair scrape across the floor.

"Damn, you done, too?" I asked.

"Yes. I'm gonna clean up in here, and then I need to finish up with the Thanksgiving menu," she explained.

"I told you I can have it catered."

"Nah, I wanna cook."

"A'ight. Hey, I'll clean up. Go do your thing, baby."

She returned to the table, leaning in to kiss me. As she backed away, I pulled her closer to me.

"Ewwwwww! Y'all gonna be kissing and stuff now?!" That was Junior, who grabbed his cup from the table, bouncing out of the kitchen with it before Nuri or I could say a word in response.

She and I stared at each other for a moment before we locked mouths again, finishing our kiss.

"Hey, I want us to try something," Nuri said into my chest. We were in bed, our bodies so close that it didn't make sense.

With my chin resting on the top of her head, I uttered, "What? You wanna try anal?"

"That would be a hell no."

I laughed, squeezing her to me. "It's like that, baby?"

"It's *absolutely* like that. I mean, have you seen your dick?"

"You have a point. So, what's up?"

"Okay, I want us to know more about each other. Like, we've been having all this excellent sex—"

"It's magnificent, per-fucking-fection."

"I know, right? So anyway, do you realize we don't know each other's middle names?"

"It's Rashad. Maleek means ruler. Rashad means good judgement."

"So, you're a ruler with good judgement. That tracks. I like it! Mine is Sublime. Nuri means light. Sublime basically means exalted or excellence."

Rolling her onto her back and settling between her thighs, I said, "Now, that *definitely* tracks. You are my light, my excellent light, Nuri Sublime Knox." Then I kissed her.

"Thank you, Maleek Rashad. So, I think every night when we go to bed, we should share something or some *things* about ourselves."

Reaching between us, I rubbed her clit, making her whimper as I shared, "Okay...my birthday is February eighth. Aquarius."

"Ooooh, shit! Mine is-is-is September twenty-fifth. Li-Li-Libra," she whined.

I grasped my dick, rubbing it between her wet folds. "Damn, I... uh, fuck! I missed your birthday?"

Lifting her head, she kissed me, her, "Mmhmm," muffled.

Sliding inside her, I squeezed my eyes shut, thinking that I'd never get used to how good she felt. "Baby, you feel so fucking good to me. I wish I could be inside you twenty-four-seven. I love fucking you."

I kissed her, rocked in and out of her, and at one point, I actually cried. I'd lost count of how many scrapes and cuts and bruises I'd acquired over the years playing hockey, and here I was crying over pussy. Granted, it was stellar, Michelin Star, James Beard Award caliber pussy, but it was pussy, nonetheless. Then again, maybe it was more than her pussy. Maybe it was her, her excellent light. Maybe I was in love with Nuri, but wasn't it too soon for that? Was there a proper time frame for falling in love? It didn't happen in the seven years I spent with Tasha. It'd only been weeks with Nuri. Nevertheless, I felt *something* for her. Something strong and undeniable, something I never wanted to stop feeling, and as she threw her head back, her mouth in an "O" as her pussy rhythmically squeezed my dick, I rode the wave of my own release.

Later, as I held her in my arms again, I spoke into the darkness, "I gotta get you a birthday gift."

Groggily, she replied, "You already did. You gave me *you*."

NURI

This was getting out of hand. Not only was he still paying me to take care of the kids, but now he was basically throwing gifts at me—a bar necklace with my name on it, a ridiculous diamond ring, his debit card. Yes, the negro gave me his *debit card*. And then...

"What's this?" I asked, staring at the keys he was holding out to me.

"Keys. To a vehicle. *Your* vehicle," he replied.

"No, my keys are in my pocket because I need to pick the kids up soon."

"That's your old car. These are for your new car. Well, it's got a few miles on it, but you're the first owner."

"But...huh?"

"I missed your birthday."

"Maleek," I groaned.

Reaching for my hand, he said, "Come look."

I took his hand, tried not to think of the things that same hand had done to me, and followed him out the kitchen, all the way to the front door. He opened it, and there parked on the semicircular driveway, right in front of the house, sat an electric blue Chevy Tahoe.

"I remembered you told me your favorite color is blue. Your name is on the plate. You like it?" he asked.

"Close the door," I said, my eyes glued to the truck.

"What?"

"Close the door."

"O...kay."

Once the door was closed, I fell to my knees in front of him, frantically tugging at the waist of his sweats. Once his dick was free, I did my best to swallow that motherfucker whole.

"Oh, fuck!" he yelled. "Nuri...shit!"

The next day, I let go of my apartment.

25

MALEEK

I didn't understand love before Nuri.
Now, I do.

26

NURI

"Why are you staring at me?" I asked as I stood in the bathroom trying to get my edges right.

"Your hair. It's so beautiful. What kind of braids are those?" Maleek queried as he leaned against the wall behind me.

"Knotless," I informed him.

He left the wall and was right behind me in seconds, his hands on my waist, his mouth on my neck. "You know what my favorite thing about you is?"

"My pussy?"

He chuckled, his warm breath tickling the skin of my neck. "Close, but no."

"Gotta be my ass."

"I do love your ass, but no. It's your smile. That smile of yours makes me want to give you the world."

Gazing at him in the mirror, I said, "You do that every day. Now, leave me alone before we end up naked in here. We got guests coming."

"Fine," he groaned, swatting my booty as he left the bathroom.

MALEEK

The Sires had a game on Thanksgiving, so we celebrated on the day before. I sent a car for my mom, making her the first to arrive. She looked beautiful in a dark green dress and a long black coat. Her Afro was cut short, and she wore a little makeup. She looked happy to see me, and as she eyed the foyer with wonder, I felt like shit for not showing her my house sooner.

"Oh, Maleek! This is a gorgeous house! So big! Plenty of room for the kids!" she marveled.

Grasping her hand, I agreed, "Yes, ma'am. You ready to meet them?"

"You know I am!"

"Maleek, who was at the door?" Nuri yelled from somewhere. Presumably, the kitchen.

"My mom! Come meet her," I called back.

When Nuri stepped into the foyer in a black dress that somehow wrapped around her body, my mouth fell open like I hadn't watched her shimmy into it earlier. She was so fucking stunning to me. Pure perfection.

I had to shake myself out of a semi-trance to say, "Ma, this is Nuri Knox. Nuri, this is my mom, Iesha Elliott."

"Oh, you're gorgeous, and I don't shake hands; I hug!" my mom chimed, grabbing Nuri's proffered hand and pulling her into an embrace.

I smiled as Nuri let out a giggled, "Yes, ma'am."

Nuri and my mom had similar body types. I hadn't realized it before that moment.

Releasing my lady, my mother backed up and inspected her. "She is sunshine. I can see it all over her. She's glorious! I know she's good with the kids."

I nodded, moving closer to Nuri and wrapping an arm around her waist. "She is, and she's good with me, too."

My mother's eyes expanded along with her smile. "Ooooh, I see, and I love it! She's the one, Poo-Bear. She's definitely the one. You both have love written all over you. Now, let me meet these kids."

As I moved to show my mom to the living room, Nuri muttered, "Poo-Bear?"

"Shut up," I hissed, making her laugh.

We had a full house. Rapp, his girl, Ford, my mom, Nuri's girl Coco, my home's usual residents, and for some reason, Robin Stick, filled my abode with chatter and laughter, and I loved it. My mother quickly hit it off with the kids, which didn't surprise me. If children were as intuitive as I always heard they were, I knew they sensed nothing but goodness from Iesha Elliott. Only a woman like my mom would be excited about meeting her ex's kids by another woman. Plus, Jules and Junior were masters at going with the flow. New care-giver? Check! New home? Check! More new people? Check! Dr. Rice told me their ability to easily adjust was a trauma response, their way of keeping themselves from being a bother. Evidently, this response was developed while they lived with their parents. We still weren't exactly sure what their lives were like before my father and stepmom passed because the whole process of therapy was excruci-atingly slow, and per Dr. Rice, took the utmost patience. We did know the kids spent a lot of time alone and were emotionally neglected. In some ways, physically, too...even in a two-parent home. That was wild to me!

"Aye, Jones...I see why you been bippity bopping around and shit 'cause gah-ah-ahhhh dayum! Yo' woman fine as seven thousand motherfuckers! That ass! Pussy prolly hot as a natural-gas space heater!" Ford whispered. He was standing beside me at the kitchen counter as we both refilled our plates. Nuri had showed out—ham, turkey, dressing, greens, yams, potato salad, a damn pound cake, shit! "Shiddddd, I know she got that wishing well kiss and tell pussy!" he added.

His words made me stop in the middle of dishing more dressing onto my plate. "Nigga, I will knock every tooth out your head, break both your legs, and stab you in the throat with a hot knife *after* cutting your tongue out your mouth if you *ever* say some shit like that about my woman again."

"Damn! A'ight, man. I was just saying...she pressure, my guy. Pah-ressure! That's all."

"You think I don't know that? Mark-ass..."

"Ole violent ass nigga. Shit!" Ford muttered as he headed back into the dining room.

"Ford musta said some out-of-line shit about Nuri," Rapp surmised, taking Ford's place in the re-up line.

"Ford gon' make me beat the shit out of him. That's what he gon' do."

"Heard. So, I gotta say, she's definitely a good look for you. You're a whole different dude with her. You look genuinely happy."

I glanced at him and nodded. "I am. She's special. I can already see forever with her. No question that I'd wife her."

"Damn, you just got with her."

I shrugged. "When you know, you know. I just figured that shit out myself. I thought being apprehensive and hesitant was normal. I guess you can get used to anything."

"Yeah, I hear you."

I smacked Rapp's shoulder and headed back to the dining room, reclaiming my seat next to my lady and leaning in to kiss her cheek. She smiled before kissing me in the mouth.

So, I whispered, "Keep on and you gon' get fucked."

Her eyes ballooned. "We have a house full of people."

I lifted my eyebrows. "This is a big house. We can find some privacy."

"Stop," she grunted.

"Fine, just know I'ma fuck the 'i' off your name tonight."

Nuri spit out the water she was drinking.

"Maleek, are you over there being naughty?" my mom asked.

I grinned and shrugged.

"Miss Iesha, they be kissing all the time! Hugging, too!" Junior reported, his nose scrunched up. Jules nodded in agreement.

"My PYT, Coco, do you like to hug and kiss?" Leo, AKA Robin Stick, asked with a silly grin on his face. I was beginning to wonder how his ass was getting all that play myself. Cornball. He'd been up Coco's ass since she arrived. Dude was blond-haired, green-eyed, pale as hell, and loved him some black women. Coco was cute, thick like Nuri but taller and lighter skinned, with a wild purple Afro. She was different. Really nice, though.

"I dooooo!" Coco twittered.

"You should come to our game tomorrow. Be my guest," Stick offered.

"I was going with Nuri and the kids anyway, so I'll be there."

"You wanna kiss Miss Coco, don't you, Mr. Stick? Ewwwww!" Junior yelled through a mouthful of food.

"Junior, what did I tell you about talking with your mouth full?" Nuri fussed.

"Sowwy," Junior garbled, making Nuri sigh.

I looked around the table to see that Ford was concentrating on stuffing his face. I still wanted to kick his ass, though. Rapp and his girl were engaged in a quiet, and what looked to be, intense conversation. My mom was saying something to Jules, both of them smiling.

Then, Nuri's hand met my thigh as she leaned in to whisper, "I love this."

I turned to face her, taking in her beauty. "Me, too...and I love you."

She blinked, surprise in her eyes before she softly returned, "I love you, too...Poo-bear."

The doorbell stopped me from threatening to fuck the "r" off her name. "Let me go get this," I said, leaving the table and wondering who it could be.

When I checked the peephole, my shoulders dropped on their own.

It was Tasha.

27

MALEEK

She looked good, as usual, inky black hair—all hers—framing her oval face and cascading past her shoulders in waves, eyebrows perfectly manicured, flawless makeup, dressed in tight gold leggings and a sheer white blouse, gold fingernails to match her gold stilettos. I used to rack my brain trying to figure out why I couldn't just *make* myself love her. After all, she was what most men would consider the total package. Now, I understood how that was an impossibility for me. She wasn't Nuri, *my one*. It really was that simple.

"You look good," she said, eyeing me from head to toe.

Glancing down at the black turtleneck and black jeans I wore, I shrugged. "Thanks. You, too. Uh...what's up?"

"Um, I know you have a game tomorrow, so you're probably observing the holiday today with your...siblings." It sounded like it literally hurt her to say that last word.

"Uh-huh," I confirmed.

"Yeah, so I was thinking maybe you and I could go grab a drink or something. I know there are a couple bars open tonight."

"Tash—"

"Hey, who is it?" That was Nuri, her boisterous voice fading as she reached the open door, stepping beside me with an, "Oh."

"Oh, good! Nasheeka is here. She can watch the kids for you while we go out."

"What?" Nuri snapped. "Where y'all going, *Maleek*?"

Aw, hell.

I turned and whispered directly in Nuri's ear, "Nowhere. Give me a minute...please?"

Without a word, Nuri left the foyer, and I sighed before returning my attention to Tasha. "Hey, you gotta go, Tash."

"Damn, she's acting like you're her man or something. Fucking weirdo. I always thought she was strange. Who quits teaching and leaves all those benefits behind to become a nanny?" Tasha muttered.

"Tash, did you hear me? You gotta go."

"Why? Because that obese weirdo thinks you're her man?"

"No, because I *am* her man."

Tasha just stood there, first frowning in what appeared to be confusion, a frown that eventually slid into a scowl. "I know you fuckin' lyin'! I *know* you didn't just tell me that one, you've already started another relationship, and two, it's with the fucking help! You have got to be playing! Like, be so fucking for real, Maleek!"

"I'm not playing, and as much as I respect you, I'm not going to stand here and listen to you talk shit about her."

Her hand flew up, but I caught it before it landed on my face. "Leave, Tasha. *Now*," I growled.

Snatching away from me, she spat, "Fuck you! You never deserved me anyway with your unlearned dick!"

As soon as she turned to leave, I shut and locked the front door, taking a minute to shake that confrontation off before returning to my white-ass dining room. I needed to do some redecorating.

NURI

I watched him enter our bedroom and head straight for the bath-room. I was burrowed under the covers in a t-shirt and panties, exhausted from the day's festivities. When he finally emerged in nothing but those crisp white boxers he always wore—he had to own a million pairs of them—I asked, "Your mom good?"

"Yep. She's very comfortable in the guest room. So is Jules," he replied, climbing in bed and immediately pulling me to him.

"Jules was not playing about wanting your mom to spend the night or staying in the room with her, huh?"

"Nope. I ain't heard Jules speak that many words since she's been here!"

"Well, I can see why she likes Miss Iesha. She's so sweet."

"Always has been. Sorry it took so long for you to meet her."

"It actually didn't take long. It's just that everything else about us happened so fast."

Silence until he said, "Does that bother you? The fact that we've been moving fast, I mean. I promise this ain't a rebound thing, Nuri. I wasn't a real part of that relationship with Tasha for years before she left. That shit she was saying about us going out? She's just used to running things. I let her because...fuck, I don't know. I guess it was easy to let her control something I didn't want anyway. I was...I hate letting people down. I was always afraid of disappointing her. I guess I believed I owed her."

"Owed her for what?" I enquired.

"For her loyalty, for choosing me and sticking with me despite me being...me."

I was facing his chest, my heart aching at the strain in his voice. "But you're wonderful. Who *wouldn't* choose you?"

"You ain't pay attention to that picture that used to hang in the living room? You didn't see how scraggly I looked?"

"You looked young, still cute though."

"Nah, I looked basic, and besides that, I was...and still am...a little messed up mentally..."

He went on to tell me how his father essentially removed him from his life, to which I replied, "I'm sorry, baby," as I kissed his chest. "So that's why you didn't know Junior and Jules until now?"

"Yeah."

"It's weird, though, because the way Junior talks, your father really admired you."

"I know, and that's confusing the shit out of me. He put me down as his preferred guardian for them, too. Like, why?"

"Maybe...maybe he had regrets. I think he really loved you and regretted not being in your life."

"Why he ain't reach out then?" he said, sounding very similar to how I imagined he did as a teen.

"I don't know. Some people just can't seem to get it together enough to confront the hard stuff, you know? Whether it's embarrassment or fear of rejection, some people can't handle grown-up shit."

"Guess he passed that down to me. I definitely didn't handle my shit when it came to me and Tasha. I just let stuff happen. I promise not to be that way with you. I want you to want me forever like I want you. I want us to work."

"You really want me forever?" I asked.

"Yes. I do, baby."

"I want that, too."

"Then let's make it happen."

MALEEK

The next morning, Nuri and I awoke to the heavenly aroma of breakfast filling our huge home. My mom had cooked and was fixing the kids' plates as they eagerly waited.

As we stood observing the scene, Nuri gushed, "Wow! This is a crazy spread!"

And it was—French toast, bacon, scrambled eggs, sausage, cheesy grits, damn!

"I don't know if we're gonna be able to let you leave, Miss Iesha," Nuri continued, and judging by the grin on Jules' face as she dug into her plate, I'd say she agreed.

A week or so later, my mom officially moved in with us, gladly and eagerly helping with the kids, cooking dinner, and so on. I liked having her around. So did Nuri. It was crazy, though. I'd spent a lot of time both loving my mother and being angry at her. Loving her kindness and nurturing of me and hating what I saw as her weakness, her meekness, her proclivity for being taken advantage of. These were things I believed she'd passed down to me, but now, I saw everything in a new light. My mom was good. She was also strong. While she did let people run over her for a time, it was those people who should've been the main targets of my animosity, not her. I loved her kindness, the same kindness that attracted me to Nuri.

"You sure about this?" she asked as I loaded her suitcases into my Jeep.

I climbed into the driver's seat and glanced over at her. "Why? You changed your mind or something?"

"No, no. I love being there with the kids. I just don't want to be a bother."

"You could never be a bother to me. Plus, I haven't seen you this happy in a long time."

"It's the kids. They give me purpose."

Leaning in to kiss her cheek, I said, "I love you, Ma, and I'm sorry I haven't been a better son. I just..."

Resting a hand on my cheek, she gave me a smile, tears shimmering in her eyes. "Oh, Maleek...baby, you don't owe me any apologies. Dealing with my illness was a lot, too much for a little boy. You have been the best son I could ask for. The best. Hey, you still like chicken spaghetti?"

I nodded, flashing her a smile. "Yes, ma'am...I do. Only yours, though."

"I'll make you some. Wanna stop by the store so I can get the ingredients?"

"Nuri and I are supposed to go grocery shopping when I get home. Text me a list."

"Okay, baby."

———

Nate: *I haven't heard from you in a while. Everything okay? You and Tasha back together?*

I answered my agent's text with: *Everything is good. Me and Tasha are over.*

Nate: *Oh, okay. How you dealing?*

Me: *I'm great, got a new lady. The kids are good. No complaints.*

Nate: *Good! Now check your email. I sent you a contract.*

I knew he'd been working on a deal for this line of neckties made by a Black designer. I was supposed to start wearing them on game days. They were dope, too.

Me: *Will do.*

I received another message as I sent that last one to Nate.

Ford: *Just checking to see how Nuri is doing. Tell her I said hi.*

Me: *(Middle finger emoji)*

Ford. *Lolololol*

I left that text string and moved on to another.

Rapp: *I broke up with Indira.*

Me: *Damn. Why? What happened?*

Rapp: *Thanksgiving happened. You're a different person with Nuri than you were with Tasha. I want what you got now. I didn't have that with Indira.*

Me: *I get it. I hope you find your one soon.*

Rapp: *Yeah, me too.*

A message came in from Robin Stick, of all people.

Stick: *Jones! Coco said I'm fine as frog hair. What does that mean?*

I heard that shit in his French-Canadian accent, too. Laughing, I sent: *It means you're in there, my guy!*

Stick: *Oh! Thank you, mane!*

Mane? This cornball...

Moving on, I sighed at the string of messages from my ex.

Tasha: *Were you fucking that Nonnie bitch while we were together?*

Tasha: *Did you know her when I hired her? Had you already been fucking her?*

Tasha: *Why HER?*

Tasha: *I shouldn't have left you. I'm sorry.*

Tasha: *Is that why you started fucking her? Because I left?*

Tasha: *You said you understood how I felt.*

Tasha: *How could you move on so fast?!*

Me: *Tash, I'm not trying to hurt you. I should've ended things a while ago. You deserved better.*

Tasha: *I know I deserved better!*

Tasha: *Fuck you, bitch!*

Scratching my forehead, I decided to block her. Trying to reason with her was a waste of time.

Then I got a message from Nuri: *I was thinking. Anal is still out but I wouldn't mind a finger in my ass.*

I smiled.

Me: *Can I eat your ass?*

Nuri: *Oh, yes! I wanna try that too!*

Man, I loved the shit out of her.

Nuri: *I need to know something, though.*

Me: *What's up?*

Nuri: *Why are we texting each other when we're in bed together?*

Me: *I don't know. You started it this time.*

Nuri: *Right. I was jealous.*

"Jealous of what?" I said, placing my phone on the nightstand and turning the lamp off.

"You were having too much fun with your phone," she explained.

"You were in your phone, too."

"So?"

I grinned, taking her phone out of her hand and placing it next to mine. Then I gathered her naked body in my arms and kissed her before saying, "I got your ass spoiled, don't I?"

"Yep."

Chuckling, I proposed, "Let me see if I can spoil you some more."

In seconds, my face was between her thighs—my favorite place.

28

MALEEK

"Do either of you have anything on your mind? Any worries you'd like to share with Maleek and I?" Dr. Rice asked.

Junior's head shot up.

"Go ahead, Junior," she urged.

The four of us were on our cushions on the floor in a semi-circle in Dr. Rice's office. Junior sat across from me. Jules was in her regular spot right next to me.

"I just wanna say that I still like living with you, Maleek. I thought I would stop liking it when Miss Nuri started being your girlfriend, but I didn't."

I frowned, glancing at Dr. Rice, who nodded at me. "Why?" I asked. "I thought you liked Nuri?"

"I do! I like her a lot. I just thought you and her would be like Mommy and Daddy were."

"How were they?" I questioned.

He shrugged. "They liked each other a lot, but they didn't like me and Jules that much."

"Why do you say that, Junior?" Dr. Rice probed.

"Because we heard them say it. Didn't we, Jules? You remember, don't you?" Junior said.

Little Jules looked up at me and nodded, softly confirming with, "They were fighting about something, and Daddy said Mommy was right and that having kids, uh...ruined everything. I was hiding, but I heard them."

"Hiding, like in that picture you drew?" I asked.

"Mmhmm, and Mommy said I was an accident," Jules provided.

My heart stuttered at the thought of them hearing those things. If their mother was still alive when it happened, that would mean they were like nine and six years old at the most.

Damn.

"How did hearing that make you guys feel?" Dr. Rice asked.

"Sad," Jules shared.

"Yeah," Junior concurred. "They didn't like us. I could tell before they said it, though."

"How?" I queried, my voice strained. This shit was breaking my heart. Having our father in their lives was as bad for them as me being dismissed by him.

"They would get mad if we talked to them. They didn't like for us to be out of our rooms. It wasn't like it is with you and Miss Nuri. I can tell y'all like having us around," Junior said.

Jules grabbed my hand and nodded in agreement.

"Is that why you don't like to talk, Jules?" I asked, trying not to fucking cry.

"Uh-huh," she replied.

"Yeah, people kept saying she stopped talking after Daddy died, but Jules didn't really talk to anyone but me before that unless she was at school. She *had* to talk at school," Junior supplied.

"Well, I want you two to know that I *do* like having you around. I...I love y'all," I said, the revelation hitting me just as I spoke it. I did love them, and after just a few months of knowing them, I couldn't imagine my life without them in it. Jules, Junior, and Nuri were everything to me.

"I love you, too," they both said out of sync with Jules leaning into me, and I spent the remainder of their therapy session continuing to fight tears.

NURI

"This is so exciting!" Miss Iesha gushed as we settled in our seats at the glass. The Sires were playing at home, and it was a Friday night. Miss Iesha seemed almost as excited as the kids were to be there.

"It is! When was the last time you attended one of Maleek's games?" I asked.

"Hmm," she said as she pulled Jules's skull cap down over her ears. "I think he was in high school."

"Really?" I squeaked.

"Yes, I fell into a pit when he went off to college. I was so depressed for so long that I barely remember those years. Felt like I was losing him. I wasn't, of course. I just...I was a mess. So, I missed those games. I usually watch his professional games on TV."

"You're feeling better now, right?"

"Oh, yes! They finally put me on some medicine I can tolerate. I feel great most days. I still get down, but being with y'all, helping with the kids? It's kind of given me a purpose."

"I'm glad, and we love having you with us."

She smiled at me as Jules leaned into her. "Nuri, I want to thank you for helping my boy, for making him happy. He went through a lot dealing with my ups and downs, and then...did he tell you about—" She lowered her voice to a whisper. "—how his father treated him?"

I nodded. "Yes, ma'am...he did."

"So, you see, he didn't have much along the lines of parental support. Initially, I thought Tasha was good for him, and maybe she was for a time, but I don't think their relationship was supposed to last as long as it did. I suppose it's my fault he held on to it for so long."

"Why do you say that?" I asked, my eyebrows knitted in genuine confusion.

"Stability. He didn't have that with me or his father—I guess that means his father was to blame, too—but he had it with Tasha. She was always there for him, by his side."

I nodded, understanding. "Until she wasn't."

"Yes. I believe that if she stayed with him, he never would have left because he appreciated her."

"Yeah."

"Hey, I'm about to make a food run. Place your orders!" That was Coco, who was wearing a replica of her new man, Robin Stick's, jersey and a big goofy grin on her face.

Junior piped up first. "Pizza!"

Miss Iesha knew hockey.

Like, she *knew it* knew it, and she was mad vocal during the game, hopping up, screaming, and making me flinch more than once. By then, I knew a lot more about the sport, myself, enough that I actually understood most of what was happening.

Miss Iesha took the kids to the restroom during the first intermission. By the second intermission, *I* needed the restroom. So, I left Junior and Jules in her capable hands and Coco's semi capable hands. I hated public restrooms and was an expert at holding my pee, but evidently, I had too much soda during the game.

I'd finished my business and was washing my hands when I heard, "I never would've guessed it. I really thought you were the safe choice."

My head snapped up from the sink to see Tasha in the reflection of the restroom mirror. She was standing behind me wearing a scowl and a Maleek Jones jersey.

With wide eyes, I spun around, my hands still wet. "What the fuck?!" I shrieked.

"Seven years. Seven damn years and you step in and ruin it all! You and those fucking kids!" Tasha yelled.

"Look, I can totally understand why you're upset about losing him. *Totally.* But you left, didn't you? Don't blame me for your stupidity."

She looked shocked. Yes, I was nice, but I wasn't a damn doormat. Not for her, anyway.

She flew into my face, and I stared up at her, unflinching in my stance.

"I'm going to get him back. When he realizes I'm the one he wants, he will drop your fat ass in a second!"

I put my hand in her face. "First of all, back the fuck up. Second, if that should happen, if by chance the two of you end up together again, *which I highly doubt,* and you kiss him, be sure to tell me how my pussy tastes because he *stays* eating it."

Her mouth hung open as I pushed past her to exit the restroom.

"She did *what*?!" Maleek bellowed, dropping his duffel bag on the bedroom floor with force. I'd texted him about the weird-ass confrontation with Tasha, and this was how he greeted me when he made it home after the game.

"Baby, you gotta calm down. You're gonna wake the whole house up," I tried, but he was too keyed up.

"What did you say she did?!" he yelled.

"She confronted me in the restroom, got all up in my face talking shit. She's convinced you're going to leave me. I know better, but it was weird. She's unhinged."

"Yeah, and so am I when it comes to you. I'll be right back," he growled, turning to leave the room.

"Wait! Where are you going?" I shrieked.

He didn't answer, so I said, "Maleek, where *the fuck* are you going?"

Holding the doorknob, he sighed. "Tasha's mom's house. She was out of line. She had no business messing with you. Ain't nobody bothered her ass. We just over here living life. Damn!"

"In a house *she* picked out. This was *her* life. I'm living the life *she* wanted. You were her everything for seven years. No, she shouldn't have messed with me, but I get it. I'd probably be just as crazy if things ended between us. Let it go. I'm fine. I was just letting you know what happened."

He was silent for a good while, his back to me as he stood at the door. When he turned around, concern filled his eyes. "I don't want her to run you away from me. I...I need you. I love you."

"She *can't* run me away from you. No one can. I'm good, and she might be taller than me, but I can kick her ass."

He smiled. "I believe it. I'm sorry for yelling and shit."

"It's okay. Come here."

He walked over to where I sat on his side of the bed, squatting in front of me.

Reaching down to cradle his handsome face in my hands, I told him, "I love you. You know that?"

"I do. I love you, too, baby. So damn much," he professed.

We kissed, and when our lips parted, he said, "I'm going to ask my mom to watch the kids tomorrow. I wanna take you somewhere, spend the whole day with you. We've never gone out, just the two of us, for more than a few hours."

I grinned. "Okay."

"And pack a bag."

"Oh, so it's gonna be an all nighter? Yes!"

29

NURI

I rolled my ass to the beat of Cardi B's *Up* as Maleek smacked it, making me giggle. We were at this bougie nightclub called *Plush-St. Louis*, acting ratchet as hell, and I loved it. Spinning around to face him, I yelped when he grabbed me at the waist, pulling my body into his.

With his mouth on my ear, he asked, "Do you have any idea how fucking sexy you are?"

Smiling, I replied into his ear, "I do, but tell me anyway."

He answered me by covering my mouth with his, kissing me so deeply that I forgot we were in public. I also forgot my name, address, and zip code. I would've legit been hard pressed to recite the alphabet if asked to do so. One of his big hands held me at the waist while the other grasped my ass cheek tightly. I could feel the vibration of his moans as we kissed for long minutes, savoring the taste of each other right there on the dance floor.

Breaking our connection, his eyelids heavy, he clutched my hand in his. "Come on."

I knew where he was leading me, and I knew why he was leading me there. I'd felt his hardness during the kiss, hardness that had me wet with anticipation. We boarded the elevator and stared at each other before we both started smiling. By the time we stepped into our VIP suite, we were laughing at nothing. We were just happy.

So happy.

In quick succession, my ruched red skirt was up around my waist, I was bent over the back of the black sectional sofa, and Maleek's face was between my ass cheeks, his tongue lavishing my actual asshole. The mere fact that he was doing this, that he was licking my literal ass, made me want to scream. It was so nasty. So *over the top* nasty.

I loved it.

His mouth left me, and I whimpered, "Maleek..."

No sooner than that word left my lips did I feel his finger in my ass and his dick in my pussy.

"Ohhhh, shit!" I hissed.

"You know this my pussy, right?" he asked, his voice rough.

"Mmhmmm," I hummed, finding it hard to concentrate on forming actual words.

"Then say it, baby. Tell me it's mine."

"It's your pussy. All yours, shit!"

His body was crowding my back as he said, "That's right. *All* mine."

"Hey, Nuri. You know Mother Dear's birthday is coming up and we're planning the annual party. I'm sure you'll want to be there, like always. It'll be at her house, as usual. Let me know what you plan on bringing. Okay, bye!"

I pulled the phone from my ear and closed my eyes. The voice message was from Aunt Yvette. I loved celebrating my grandma's birthday every year with the family as much as I hated it. My people were hard to deal with to say the least. That wasn't a fair statement.

It wasn't my people as a whole. It was my aunt who was problematic, but she was enough.

"Why you over there frowning?" Maleek asked. We were in bed, and I shouldn't have been checking my phone, but I was.

"Got a voicemail from my aunt," I told him, my eyes on the ceiling.

"Bad news?"

"No...my grandmother's birthday is coming up. My family always throws a big party for her."

"The grandmother who raised you?" he queried. I hadn't told him much about my family, but I had shared my love for my late grandmother.

"Yes. My aunt was reminding me of the party."

"And...you don't want to go?"

"I do and I don't. My family is...different. I don't really enjoy being around some of them, but I'd love to be in my grandmother's house again. I feel closest to her there. Coco usually goes to the party with me, you know, as a buffer, but she's so wrapped up in Robin Stick. I doubt she'll be available."

"I can go with you, depending on when it is and whether or not I have a game."

Flipping over to face him, I chimed, "Really?"

"Yeah. I got you. Always and forever."

I wanted to cry, but instead, I kissed him long and slow.

Once our mouths disconnected, he said, "Now, put that phone up so we can enjoy the rest of the night. I ain't spend all that money on this suite for you to be in your phone."

Grinning, I tossed my phone on the floor. We had a great day out and about. Now, we were in a gorgeous hotel room with free time to explore each other's bodies and be as loud as we wanted.

"Yes, sir...Mr. Jones," I said.

MALEEK

I was as tired as I was happy after a whole day with no one but my Light. We shopped, ate at this restaurant called *Bait*, danced, and fucked until I legit could barely walk the next morning. Nuri had a little limp going on, too, as we left our suite and boarded the elevator. I had our luggage—my duffel on my shoulder and her rolling suitcase handle in my hand. As soon as the doors closed and the box began to descend, I was on her, kissing her, sucking her neck, my ears filled with the sound of her laughter. We were both so damn happy, elated. I'd honestly never been as happy in my entire life.

"I love you," I murmured, my mouth hovering over hers as I held her face in my hands.

"Almost as much as I love you, Mr. Jones," she responded, her eyes on my mouth.

"Nah, ain't no way you got more love for me than I got for you. No way. Not with as much pussy as I be eating."

Her eyes lifted to meet mine, amusement evident in them. "What does you eating my pussy have to do with you loving me?"

"Nothing."

We were both laughing when we exited the elevator, hands joined as we headed toward the desk to check out.

"About damn time! Ain't that much fucking in the world!"

Nuri and I both halted in our tracks and turned around. What in the whole, entire, complete, and utter fuck? What was Tasha doing there? And from what she said, she'd been waiting on us.

The hell?

"Tasha...what the fuck?" I said, frowning so deeply that my head was beginning to hurt. "Did you follow us here?"

Hands on her hips, she gave me a smirk. "No, *dumbass*. I put a tracker on your car years ago. I always know where you are. Had to protect my investment and you definitely proved yourself to be untrustworthy."

"A tracker?! You are out of your fucking mind!"

"I'm out of my mind? *I'm out of my mind?!* You're the one using the skills I taught you to eat another woman's pussy while you're engaged to *me*! In *my* house! In *my* damn bed!"

"Nah, he got us a new bed," Nuri muttered, "at my request."

"Bitch, was I talking to you?" Tasha shot at her.

"You better watch who you calling a bitch, *bitch!*" Nuri hissed.

Rolling her eyes from Nuri to me, Tasha commanded, "Maleek, go get us a room so we can work things out. I'm over this shit. I want my life back! I forgive you for whatever *this* is supposed to be." She flapped her hand at Nuri.

"Awwww, you really think he's going to do that, don't you?" Nuri mocked.

"Oh, he will. You're nothing but a minor distraction. You're fooling yourself if you think he really wants to be with you. I got skin in the game. Seven fucking years!" Tasha ranted.

Scratching my forehead and well aware of the curious eyes on us in the hotel's lobby, I said, "Tash, I understand you're upset but we're over, and this shit is weird. You're making a scene in these folks' establishment. Plus, you're literally stalking us. I don't want to have to call the police, but I will. You gotta stop this shit. I'm not gonna let you keep disrespecting or harassing Nuri."

"What the fuck is that?" was how she chose to respond.

"What the fuck is *what?*" I replied, confused as shit. Tasha's ass had really lost it.

"What the fuck is that on your finger? Is that a got damn wedding band, Maleek?!"

I squeezed Nuri's hand and slowly said, "Yeah. It is. Me and Nuri are married."

30

NURI

TWO WEEKS EARLIER...

"You ready?" he asked, peeping in the bedroom.

"Yeah," I said, looking down at the jeans and plain white t-shirt I had on. "I'm ready. You seem extra hyped about going grocery shopping today. What's that about?"

"I'm always hyped to spend time with you. Come on."

We left in his Jeep, with him keeping one hand on the steering wheel and the other on my thigh. The weather was nice out, the coldness that'd had our city under siege having eased on this December day. Our plan was to get the grocery shopping done, grab lunch, and head home. Hopefully, we'd have some time to chill before we headed back out to pick the kids up from school. Maleek had an early morning practice and no game or meetings that day, so it was one of those rare times when he got to be home with us uninterrupted.

"You got your mom's stuff?" I thought to ask, remembering he had taken her to pick up some of her clothes.

"Yeah. Oh, she texted me some things we need to pick up at the store. She's cooking chicken spaghetti tonight," he informed me.

"Ohhh, okay. That sounds good!"

"It is."

I closed my eyes and smiled. I wasn't sure how long this would last, how long we'd be together, but in that moment, I was the happiest I'd been in my entire life. Being loved by and in love with this man was the stuff dreams were made of. It almost felt too good to be true, but it was real, and so was he.

I opened my eyes when I felt the Jeep pull to a stop, observing our surroundings. We were definitely not at a grocery store.

"Maleek, where are we?" I questioned, shifting my gaze to him.

He locked eyes with me before turning his attention to the windshield. "City Hall."

"Oh...you got business here or something?"

"*We* have business here, hopefully."

"What—"

"Nuri, will you marry me? I...I got the rings. I just...I love you and I want to be with you forever."

"I love you, too, but...you're sure?"

"I am."

"So, we're here to..."

"Get a marriage license."

"Okay, and then we're going to set a date? Plan a wedding?"

"No...I already did that. The date is today. We have an appointment at a wedding chapel in an hour."

My mouth fell open. "Maleek..."

"Nuri, I spent years trying to figure out what was missing in my life and in my relationship with Tasha. The only conclusion I can come up with is you. *You* were missing. You're my one, my *only* one, and if you'll have me, I want to make you my wife today. I'm more than ready and more than sure. So...will you marry me?"

Through a flood of tears, I said with inexplicable confidence and surety in my decision, "Yes. I will."

That day, I married my first love, and afterwards, we bought some groceries, picked up the kids, and celebrated our union with some bomb-ass chicken spaghetti and some late night, bomb-ass sex.

31

MALEEK

NOW...

Tasha stood stone still, eerily quiet, and the shit was spooky, for lack of a better word. I think I would've been more comfortable with her physically attacking me.

Beside me, Nuri cleared her throat, gaining my attention. "I'm gonna go get us checked out," she said into my ear.

I nodded but didn't take my eyes off Tasha as Nuri walked away. "Tash—"

"Wow. Like...woooow. Is that bitch Haitian or something? Creole? A descendent of Marie Laveau? Seriously, what the fuck is going on?"

"Tasha, I—"

She shook her head, her eyes now full of tears. "Did you ever love me, Maleek?"

"I...I had love for you, Tash. I just...I'm sorry. I should've let you go the second I realized my heart wasn't in it anymore."

"It was the kids? How I acted over them?" Her voice was small, soft, defeated.

"No. It was *me*. Like I said, I knew I needed to end things long ago. I just...didn't. I'm truly sorry. I never *ever* wanted to hurt you." *That's why I stayed with you*, I added mentally.

She nodded, wiping her wet cheeks before turning on her heels and exiting the hotel.

Once Nuri and I were outside, I searched my Jeep for the tracker in the fucking rain, found it, and threw it across the damn parking lot.

———

Nuri was sick, couldn't keep anything down, barely got out of bed, and it scared me, made me feel like I did when I was a kid and my mom would be stuck in the bed. Seeing someone I loved suffering was triggering as hell for me, made me feel powerless. On top of that, I still had to work. If it wasn't for my mama, everything would've fallen apart.

My game was suffering, but shit, my head was fucked up. I wasn't a damn machine. I was a man, a man so deeply in love that it didn't make sense. So deeply in love that seeing her like this, so listless and weak, was tearing me apart.

I had practice that morning but didn't want to leave. I wanted to climb back in bed with her and hold her all day long, but I had a whole house full of people to support.

So, I walked over to her side of the bed, smiling at the "get well" pictures from Jules and Junior that lay on the nightstand as I bent down, softly whispering, "Hey, I'm about to head out, baby."

She groggily answered, "Hmmm, okay. Be careful. Your ribs..."

There she was, sick but worried about my sore ribs, a result of me being elbowed during our last game.

"I'm good. Got my pain meds. I'll be back to help you eat lunch, okay?" I responded.

"Okay, love you."

Planting a kiss on her forehead, I told her, "Love you most."

Downstairs, I stepped into the kitchen and inhaled the breakfast my mom was cooking, gave her her daily hug and kiss, and stepped over to the table, kissing Jules' head and giving Junior dap, per his request because, and I quote, he was "too old to be kissed." Insert rolling eyes emoji.

"Hey, did you eat breakfast?" my mom asked as I moved to leave the kitchen.

"Yes, ma'am. I made a smoothie," I said.

"Okay, let me walk you to the door."

I nodded, smiling when she linked her arm with mine.

At the door, she took my face in her hands and kissed my nose. "I wanna ask you something, but I don't want to pry."

"No, ask me. What's up?" I urged her.

"Well, could Nuri be pregnant? You're married, so that's the natural course of things. You know?"

"I...she's on the pill."

She smiled. "So was I, but here you are. They're not foolproof and there isn't much of a margin for error when taking them. Just a thought." After dropping that bomb, she patted my cheek and left me standing at the front door, my mind reeling.

NURI

"Pregnant? No...I'm on—oh, shit," I mumbled.

"*Oh, shit* what?" Maleek asked, dropping onto the bed beside me, the simple action disturbing my equilibrium and making my head swim. He was just returning home from practice.

Squeezing my eyes shut, I replied, "I did miss a few pills. I kept forgetting to take them. I didn't *try* to forget..." I opened my eyes, finding his fixed on my face. "I'm sorry, Maleek."

Frowning, he asked, "Sorry for what? Ain't like you did it alone *if* that's what's going on. Also, I don't see it as a bad thing, Nuri. Do you?"

"No, I just...we've only been married for like two minutes, you're still adjusting to being your brother's and sister's guardian. Your mom just moved in. Hell, you barely know me, and now, a baby?"

"Nuri, we've been in here fucking damn near twenty-four-seven. It was bound to happen, and all that stuff you just listed? It's new for you, too. Listen, if you don't want to have it, you don't have to. I got money. We can fly to wherever and make it happen, but first, we need to know if you really are pregnant. If not, you're going to the damn ER so we can find out what's wrong because I can't take seeing you like this."

I nodded and took the box from him, a pregnancy test he'd purchased on his way home from practice.

Taking a deep breath, I stood and walked to the bathroom with my sweet husband on my heels, my heart racing, my thoughts in a confusing tangle. What was with us? Why was everything so immediate, all the events of our combined lives so successive and crowded? Would it always be like this? Could a love this wild last? I sure hoped so. I *prayed* so.

Maleek held my free hand while I peed on the stick, sat on the floor next to the toilet with his head on my knee while we awaited the results, and was the one to tell me the verdict when I couldn't make myself look.

I was pregnant. I was carrying this beautiful man's baby.

"Do you want it?" he softly asked.

Through tears, I said, "Absolutely," and right there as I sat on the toilet, he kissed me so deeply that I wondered if I was dreaming. How could life possibly be this good to little old me?

32

NURI

My first Christmas as Mrs. Jones was a blur of queasiness and simultaneous elation. It was just the family—me, Maleek, Miss Iesha, Junior, and Jules, plus a bunch of Miss Iesha's Memphis cooking that I truly wished I could enjoy, but baby wasn't having it. I'd actually lost weight since becoming pregnant, and while my doctor wasn't all that concerned, I was. At any rate, the kids loved the gifts Maleek and I ordered online for them, tons of Black Barbie stuff for Jules, Spider-Man stuff for Junior, and each of them received their very own kid-sized Sires hockey stick and helmet, plus a pair of skates. The hockey gear was definitely the highlight of the holiday for them. Seeing them jump up and down and hug their big brother, coupled with the joy on Maleek's face, made me truly happy. Together, my man and I got his mom some things off her Amazon wish list—books, shoes, and some other items, plus Maleek wrote her a huge check and gave her a replica of his jersey. She was tearfully thankful. I gave Maleek a pack of brand-new white boxers, which made him laugh, a really nice wooden watch with gears on the face that he'd mentioned he liked, and some *Marathon* gear. He loved Nipsey Hustle, RIP. He almost kissed me to death when he saw the last gift.

As for me, the kids made me some beautiful artwork, Miss Iesha gave me a gorgeous locket with one of Maleek's baby pictures inside —yes, I cried—and Maleek gave me a huge diamond ring, but the gift that made me ugly cry? It was the layout of a new home he planned to have built for us and my name alongside his on the deed to a newly purchased piece of land. If I'd had the strength, I would've sucked his dick all night long. Instead, I hugged him, kissed him, and bawled in his arms.

———

I rested my head against the passenger side window, closing my eyes and trying to keep down the little bit of food I'd eaten for breakfast and lunch. I was a month along, still sick as hell, and it was New Year's Eve, my granny's birthday. It was also arctic outside.

"You sure you feel up to this?" Maleek asked for the two-hundredth time, placing his big hand on my stomach.

"You talking to me or Poo-Bear Jr.?" I replied.

Through a chuckle, he said, "Both of y'all, but mostly you."

"I don't," I admitted, "but I want to go. I want to show you where I grew up. I want to be there for myself. That house is a healing place."

"Okay...can I ask you something, baby?"

"Yeah, of course."

"You said this is something your family does every year, right?"

"Yes, we've done it annually since she passed ten years ago."

"Okay, so why couldn't you stay with some of your folks? Why'd you have to sleep in your car?"

"Uh...the only person who actually lives in town is my Aunt Yvette. Oh, and her son, Terry. Everyone else travels in from out of town."

"So...why couldn't you stay with your aunt or cousin?"

"Because they don't like me. At least my aunt doesn't. Never has. Her son hates me by default. I probably should've contacted some of my other folks, but I didn't want to leave town. Stupid, I know."

"Nah, not stupid at all. If you'd left town, there'd be no us."

I smiled. "True, but I could've at least asked for money. I was just too embarrassed."

"Again, you probably wouldn't have answered that ad. I'm so glad you answered that ad."

"Me too, Poo-Bear."

He chuckled. "So...you said your aunt hates you? I can't imagine how or why anyone would hate you."

"Tasha does."

"Nah, she hates *me*. Not you."

"If you say so."

"Why does your aunt hate you?"

I shrugged, sitting up in my seat and glancing over at him. "She just does. My grandmother's house is unoccupied. I asked to stay there until I could get on my feet. She refused to let me."

"Damn."

"I know. It's cool, though. It's whatever."

"What about your dad, his side of the family?"

"Never knew them."

"Same, but you know that."

"Yeah."

"Your mom, she passed when you were little, right?"

"Yes, she got sick, the flu, and she had a bad reaction to an antiviral she had no idea she was allergic to. Never recovered. I was five when she passed, and then my grandmother took over raising me. We already lived with her, so it was an easy transition."

"Damn, baby...I'm sorry."

"It's all right..." We both fell quiet until I added, "My out-of-town relatives are super cool, but I haven't had much as far as family since my granny died other than Coco. She's been my ride or die since forever. I did stay with her for a bit. Couldn't deal with her psychotic-ass cats, though. If I never see those damn cats again, it'll be too soon. Fucking demons."

Maleek laughed, and so did I.

MALEEK

Her grandmother's house was located in The Ville. It was a huge, older, red-bricked façade that appeared well-kept. From what she'd told me, the house was likened to a museum. No one resided in it, but it was just as her grandmother left it, furniture and all.

Cars lined the street, most probably belonging to her family members, and as I parked, I had to smile at the look on Nuri's face, the look of a small child returning home for the first time in a long time. According to her, her grandmother was nothing short of an angel, and this place held good memories for her. She even looked like the prenatal sickness had eased a bit. I was glad because I felt terrible about how she'd been suffering.

When she reached for the door handle, I gave her a crazy look.

"My bad, I forgot!" she squeaked.

Shaking my head, I exited the truck and walked around to her side, opening the door.

"Thank you, baby," she cooed.

"You're welcome," I said, bending over to kiss her stomach. "You be good and let your mama eat," I whispered to the baby.

She was laughing when I stood to kiss her lips.

"You are so silly," she giggled.

"I know," I agreed.

Taking my hand, she led me up the concrete pathway to the front stoop. She knocked on the door and it swiftly swung open, revealing loud music and layered voices along with the unmissable aroma of good soul food. This was my kind of party!

"It's Nuri!" the woman who answered the door—I'd later learn she was a cousin of Nuri's—yelled, eliciting a chorus of, "Hey, Nuri!"

"Heyyyy," she sang in return as we stepped inside the neat house. "Everyone, this is my husband, Maleek."

"Husband?!" a woman yelled.

"What?! When you get married, girl?!" That was an older man.

"Damn, and he fine, too!" another woman shrieked, making my silly ass grin.

"Too fine!" yet another woman agreed.

In quick succession, we were herded into the formal dining room full of beautiful, dark, antique furniture, plates piled high with food were set before us, and her kin surrounded us to commence an intense interrogation of the man who cuffed their sweet Nuri. None of these people were the aunt and cousin she'd mentioned, the ones who disliked her. I was sure of that because these folks were happy to see her, happy *for* her, and extremely warm and friendly toward us both.

"Hockey? Shit, I ain't know black folks played hockey like that. They paying you good?" That question came from Nuri's Uncle Lim, her mom's brother who lived in California.

"Yes, sir. They pay me pretty well," I replied after I swallowed a mouthful of the best fried chicken I'd ever tasted in my life.

"Well, I'll be damned!"

A few minutes after I literally stuffed myself past discomfort, Nuri took me on a tour of her childhood home. Her old bedroom was on the second floor and was just as spacious as the rest of the rooms in the house. I swear, that bedroom felt like Nuri—light and airy and peaceful.

We sat together on her old bed covered in a pink patterned quilt, no words passing between us as she rested her head on my shoulder. The furniture was ancient but nice, the carpet worn but clean. It felt good to be somewhere she loved and cherished so much.

After a few minutes, I cut into the silence. "I wish I was able to meet your grandmother."

"Me too. She was so sweet and wise. She taught me so many things. I miss her every day," Nuri said.

"You look kind of like her," I said, recalling the photos I'd seen hanging in the living room. "Your mom, too."

"Yeah, I do."

"If I could've met your grandmother, I'd thank her."

She lifted her head and looked at me. "For what?"

"For raising such a special woman. You are unlike anyone I've ever met and that's what I love most about you."

She stared at me for a moment before leaning in to kiss me. "Come on. I think I can stomach some of Cousin Leah's blackberry cobbler."

"The same Cousin Leah who made that fried chicken?" I asked.

"Yep."

"Well, shit. Let's go!"

NURI

I guess I conjured Aunt Yvette up because the thought that I hadn't seen her or Terry a couple hours into our visit had just entered my mind when both appeared out of nowhere.

We were back in the dining room, me slowly trying to eat cobbler while Maleek worked his way through a plate full of desserts, countless cousins and other relatives passing in and out of the room to talk to my hockey phenom husband when I heard her voice in its usual snide tone.

"Nuri, I see you made it. They tell me you're married. Where's your husband?" she asked.

I looked up to see her standing in the doorway that connected the dining room to the kitchen. She was built like me and most of the women in our family—short and round. She was beautiful in her Kelly-green track suit, a fresh wig on her head and minimal makeup on her face. My eyes shifted to the man sitting next to me and back to her.

"He's right here. Maleek, this is my Aunt Yvette. Aunt Yvette, this is my husband, Maleek Jones," I said.

With a frown, she replied, "Oh, *this* is your husband? I was expecting someone older."

"According to Wikipedia, he's younger than her." That was Terry, who I could now see standing behind her.

"Really? When they told me you were married, I thought for sure it would be to some older man. You were looking for a home and I figured an older man would be eager to take you in," my aunt mused.

"Nope. He's not an older man," I muttered.

"I can see that. Hmmm, I guess you're more like your mother than I thought. She had a way of enchanting men. I suppose she passed that on to you."

Maleek was staring at her, his frown deepening by the second. Then he turned to me and mumbled, "The fuck?" Louder, he began, "Um, look—"

"I got it," I murmured to him before giving my attention to my aunt. "You want to go there today, Auntie? Really? You *sure* you wanna do that?"

"Are you calling yourself threatening me, Nuri?" she questioned.

"No, ma'am. I'm not, but I'm also not going to sit here and let you slander my mother just because your former husband decided to get her pregnant with me."

The room fell silent. I'd finally addressed the elephant that held prime real estate in every room my aunt and I shared probably since my birth.

"What? You don't have anything to say now? You don't want to talk about how that nasty-ass, forty-year-old man you married when you were twenty impregnated your sixteen-year-old sister, or how you begged my grandmother not to report him, or how you have treated me like some kind of cancer because I was the result of that pregnancy, *anything* other than blame a man who ended up leaving your ass despite you sticking beside him after all the shit that happened, after what he did to your little sister?!" I spat.

"Oh, shit," one of my cousins muttered.

Aunt Yvette blinked, still mute as Terry squeezed past her in the doorway. "Don't talk to my mother like that! She's your elder!"

I shook my head. "Terry, I return energy. If she wants respect from me, she better learn how to give it because I'm fucking tired of her shit. I have never done a damn thing to your mother. All I have done is exist through no fault of my own. I have ignored her attitude mostly because Mother Dear asked me to, but I have turned the other cheek long enough. She wanted to embarrass me in front of my husband, to make me feel small. Well, fuck that, fuck her, and fuck you!"

She looked shocked and so did her son. I wasn't one to go off like that, but I was sick, pregnant, and just tired of the bullshit. I watched her disappear into the kitchen with Terry on her heels, and soon, the chatter recommenced, peppered with a few more verbal reactions to our exchange.

"You wanna leave?" Maleek asked, his mouth directly on my ear.

"No," I said. "We can leave after midnight like we planned. She ain't running me out of here."

"Okay, and by the way...that was sexy as hell."

Grinning, I went back to work on my bowl of cobbler.

On the ride home, I reached over and rested a hand on Maleek's arm. "Hey, I'm sorry for not telling you about my aunt and uncle and mom before today."

He glanced at me, grasping my hand and bringing it to his thick lips. "You told me when you were ready and in the way you needed to. Shit, I enjoyed it. I like when you cuss people out. When you called Tasha a bitch? I think I came a little."

"You are a damn fool, Maleek Jones," I said once I finished laughing.

"I'm your fool, Nuri Jones."

33

MALEEK

"Dr. Martin Luther King, Jr. was born January 15, 1929, in Atlanta, Georgia. His parents' names were Michael King and Alberta King. He was a Baptist minister. He worked hard to help Black people have better lives in the United States..."

Jules was making a speech for the Sebayt House's annual Martin Luther King celebration, and she was killing it! I can't lie; I was pretty close to tears watching my baby sister share her voice with the small cafeteria full of other students and parents. Nuri sat to my left, my mom and Junior to my right, and we all wore huge smiles as she stood before the room, microphone in hand, her memorized speech flowing from her lips like a true orator. My mom had bought a sewing machine and made the red, black, and green Kente patterned dress she wore. I had forgotten my mom could sew. She was also good at crocheting and had made the baby all kinds of little yellow outfits and blankets. It was a happy moment for my little family that was stitched together like a worn quilt. We may have been assembled oddly, but we worked.

"Dr. King was a great man who left a great legacy, and that's why we celebrate his birthday every year," Jules finished, and our crew quickly stood from the uncomfortable bench, giving her a loud standing ovation.

I woke up to silence, unsure of what pulled me from a sound sleep. Had I heard something that I now couldn't remember? Later, I would realize none of my tangible senses were at work. It was my intuition, my heart, that awakened me at two in the morning to find Nuri's side of the bed empty. I lay there for a moment, still confused but also...wary, like I could feel in my bones that something wasn't right.

Visually searching the dark bedroom, I noticed light seeping from beneath the bathroom door and hoped she hadn't awakened sick again. She'd been feeling a lot better over the last couple days.

"Nuri, you okay in there?" I called through the closed door, still lying in the bed.

No response from her.

"Baby, you a'ight? Need anything?"

Still, nothing.

With a frown, I climbed out of bed, dragging myself to our ensuite bathroom in my boxers, rubbing my tired eyes with each step. Once at the door, I softly knocked and said, "Baby, you in there?" I was thinking maybe she left the bathroom but didn't turn the light off.

When I didn't get an answer this time, I grasped the shiny, silver lever handle and pushed down on it, easing the door open. My eyes quickly found her, and a panic shot through me so fast that I stumbled in the process of rushing to her. There she lay, unconscious on the floor, positioned as if she'd fallen from the toilet. Her panties were down around her ankles, and blood was everywhere—the toilet, the floor, her underwear. I scrambled to the floor, pulling her limp body into my arms, and did the only thing I could think to do.

Holding Nuri tightly to me, I yelled, "Mama! Call nine-one-one!!"

34

MALEEK

Time stood still, and I swear my heart lost its regular rhythm as I sat in that emergency room waiting to see Nuri. When I first found her like that, I thought I'd lost her, and there aren't words in any language to describe the sorrow and pain I felt. Then I thought to check for a pulse and literally started crying and wailing when I found one, so relieved that I couldn't get my shit together. Jules came to our room before my mother did, and when I heard her little voice asking what was wrong, I *really* lost it, yelling at her to go to her room. I scared the shit out of her and would have to work overtime to make it up to her, but there was no way I was going to let her see her mother figure like that. The bathroom looked like a crime scene with my Light as the victim.

She *was* a victim. She lost our baby. The doctor said she lost our baby.

"A miscarriage," he said, "is one of those things that just happen with some pregnancies."

He said the shit like he was telling me about the chance of rain in the week's forecast. Nuri, the love of my life, had lost our baby, a baby we'd already fallen madly in love with. As sick as she was, she was looking forward to the pot of gold at the end of this rainbow, the reward for all her suffering, and now...he or she was gone.

Burying my face in my hands, I battled internally with wanting to see Nuri and being unable to face her. I wanted to be there for her, to support her through this, but shit, I was hurting, too. I was hurting for her, for me, for the baby, for my mother, for Jules and Junior. We were all a part of this pregnancy. We all loved the baby.

"Mr. Jones," a voice said, the owner of which I followed through the huge ER sliding doors and through a hallway to a room. She was lying on her side, her eyes swollen as she stared at the wall beside the bed. When she noticed me, her brow wrinkled and tears began to pour from her round eyes as she sobbed, "I'm sorry. I'm so sorry. This is my fault. This is all my fault."

Hurrying to her, I held her wet face in my hands, shaking my head. "No, it's not. Don't say that. Don't even think it. This isn't anyone's fault. It just...it's just a terrible thing that happens some-times. Okay?" Yeah, I was basically parroting the damn doctor, but what he said was true. She didn't do a thing to make this happen.

She shook her head, grasping my arms as if she was afraid she'd fall through the bed or something. She pulled and tugged on me, crying so hard that she soon became hoarse, and even after that, she kept crying. There didn't seem to be any end to her tears, and as I did the best I could to comfort her, my own tears came. She didn't deserve to hurt like this. Maybe I did, but Nuri didn't.

At the breakfast table less than a week after we lost the baby, as Nuri lay in our bedroom asleep, I apologized to Jules for screaming at her that night and thought I'd literally have to beg for forgiveness, but I didn't.

"Mama Iesha said you were just scared, and you didn't mean to yell at me. She said you still love me, though," was how she responded to my apology.

"I do, Jules. I really do. You're right. I was scared, but I still shouldn't have raised my voice," I said, my speech unsteady as I glanced across the table at my mom.

Jules stood from her seat next to mine and wrapped her little arms around my neck. "It's okay. I still love you, too," she assured me. "Next time, I'll knock and wait like you said to do."

"Good deal."

As I hugged my little sister back, I mouthed, "Thank you," to my mom.

In response, she gave me a smile and a nod.

NURI

I felt different, hollow, like someone had opened me up and removed some of my vital organs, leaving behind a mountain of phantom pain where they once were. I was so unsure when I first found out I was pregnant, so scared that I'd messed up, so afraid that Maleek would somehow think I did it on purpose to trap him when I knew his beautiful heart and brain didn't work like that...*ever*. Besides, he married me before there was even an inkling of me being pregnant. He loved me. He loved our baby.

Our little girl.

As I lay in our home, in our bed, a fresh crop of tears arrived from a bottomless well, stinging my eyes before pouring down my cheeks. Yes, I was confused and unsure in the beginning, and so sick after that, that I didn't know what or how to feel, but in time, I grew excited and was so happy to be expanding our family. We all were. Now, the baby was gone and there wasn't enough evidence in the world to convince me this wasn't my fault. I *knew* it was. Maybe I didn't physically do anything to lose the baby, but it was my fault and I deserved this. Maleek, however, did not. What he deserved was someone better than me, but I loved him too much to do the right thing and let him go. I needed him too much to survive life without him, so on top of everything else, I was selfish, and I knew it.

I felt a strong arm slide over my waist and pull me backward into a hard body, my beautiful husband's body. "Hey, I'm here, baby. I'm here," he said.

I balled myself up so that only my ass touched him as I wailed into my hands.

"I know it hurts. Let it out. Just let it out," he soothed.

Why did he love me so much? Why was he constantly by my side? Why didn't he blame me?

"It's gonna get better, I promise," he continued.

"Maleek..." I cried.

"I know. I know. I got you. *I got you.* I promise I got you, baby."

I flipped over, facing him, grabbing his face and pulling it close to mine. His eyes searched mine as I stared at him, wishing I could find the right words to express my love, my guilt, my sorrow, but I had none. Not a single syllable.

So, *he* spoke. "Do you know how much I love you?"

Sniffling, I shook my head.

MALEEK

"If I had to express it in numbers, infinity wouldn't be enough. In days, eternity would fall short. In lifetimes, endless reincarnations would be just a start. I love you from somewhere deep in me that I didn't even know existed. Before you, I didn't think I *could* love. Now, I know how strongly I can. If I could take this pain from you and shoulder it all by myself, I would do it in a heartbeat. If I could manipulate time and stop it from happening, I would. I would do anything to ease your sorrow. I love you, Nuri. I love you so much I think I can feel every inch of what you're feeling, and it's killing me. I don't want this for you." By the time I ended my statement, my voice was trembling and tears were wetting my face.

"Maleek, I'm so sorry. I'm so sorry," she wept.

"You didn't do anything to be sorry for, baby."

Frantically shaking her head, she said, "No, listen. When I woke up that night, I felt off. I felt...different. I knew...I knew something was wrong, *very* wrong, and my panties were so wet that I thought I'd peed on myself. I was so embarrassed that I didn't wake you up. I didn't turn the lamp on or nothing. When I sat on the toilet and saw that it was blood, it just started gushing out at once, and I panicked. I just panicked. When the thought hit me to call your name, everything went black. I should've told you how I was feeling the moment I woke up and then maybe—"

I squeezed her body into mine. "No...no! You couldn't have done anything. You didn't cause this. You hear me? You didn't." Then I kissed her, a wet, tear-drenched kiss that took my own breath away and made me feel light-headed. With that kiss, I hoped my heart reached hers and she felt every piece of the deep love I would always have for her.

35

NURI

I'd never been one to spend a lot of time on social media. I had accounts and posted from time to time, but social media wasn't a part of my everyday life. That changed after the miscarriage. I couldn't find the strength or will to leave our bed, and on the off chance I did, I absolutely would and could not leave our room, which was odd seeing as that was the scene of the tragedy. Well, it was really the bathroom, but that was a part of the room. So, same thing. I took my meals in the bedroom when I wasn't sleeping or staring into space or crying. I knew if I left the room, I'd be nearer to my old room which had been designated the baby's nursery, and I just couldn't. I couldn't.

I spent a lot of time on hockey pages, for some reason. I guess they seemed safe. I followed the official NHL account on Instagram, as well as all the Sires players' pages and the team page along with a whole myriad of hockey-related hashtags. It was fun, mindless, and it kept me from overthinking about everything and anything. That is, until I ran across a photo posted by a page I should've unfollowed long ago.

MALEEK

I stayed glued to Nuri's side for as long as I could. The team gave me a short bereavement leave. I was allowed to miss three games before I had to return to work like our world hadn't been shattered. My mind wasn't out on that ice. I was back home with Nuri, where my heart and soul resided and nothing else mattered. No one said anything about my lackluster performance, and I was glad because I didn't want to lose my job for cussing the complete St. Louis Sires organization down to the interns working in the front office out. Shit, I was frustrated, stressed, and just plain angry enough to punch every member of the arena's janitorial crew for merely existing. The number of fights I'd been involved in during our recent games was ridiculous, but I couldn't take the damn chirping—i.e., trash talking — from our opponents, even though that was a regular and expected part of the sport.

It was all so fucking exhausting. I was running on fumes like a motherfucker, and all I thought about, all I wanted to do, was make Nuri feel better. Like everything else about our relationship, our shared pain was intense and impossible to ignore, but we loved each other. That fact was doubtless. We shared a hurricane of a love that blew through our lives and forced us together. There was no dismantling it. I was convinced of that no matter how new we were.

I made it home late that night after we managed to win this particular away game, my heart both heavy and soaring with the knowledge that my Light was only a staircase away because no matter how dim she was, she was still the sun of my universe.

I'd just entered the code in the alarm keypad when I heard my mother's voice coming presumably from the kitchen.

"Maleek, that you?"

"Yes, ma'am," I replied, walking toward her voice. "What you doing up so late?"

Sitting at the kitchen table, worry etched on her face and a mug cradled in her hands, she shared, "Something is going on with Nuri. She didn't let the kids in the room so they could watch the game with her like she promised, and you know she doesn't break promises when it comes to Jules and Junior. She wouldn't eat dinner. She's locked up in that room and refuses to tell me what's wrong."

I wasn't trying to be rude. Hell, I wasn't trying to do anything when I abruptly left the kitchen but get to my wife, racing up the stairs while telling myself not to just kick my door in. I needed to at least try knocking first. I could cuss Tasha out for choosing a house with locks on all the doors but no keys to them.

My heart was pounding as I knocked and said, "Baby, it's me. Let me in."

There was silence for a few seconds that felt like hours before I heard the lock disengage. The door inched open to reveal her retreating body in a t-shirt, her ass bouncing with every step she took. It'd been a while since we had sex, first hindered by her prenatal sickness and now by grief, and as worried as I was, my dick still jumped to attention. Ignoring it, I watched her take a seat on the foot of the bed and kneeled in front of her.

Resting a hand on her knee, I asked, "What's going on?"

She moved, sliding to the floor with me, her mouth meeting mine in a slow, sloppy kiss. Of course, I returned it. What else was I supposed to do with all that blood rushing to my dick?

When we parted, she breathily said, "Fuck me, Maleek."

"Uh...don't you want to talk?" I replied.

"No," she whispered, kissing me again as she pushed me until I was on my back on the floor. Then she was fumbling with the waist of my sweats, and before my brain could process what was happening, I was in her mouth.

"Ahhh, shit!" I groaned. "Nuri...baby...I missed you."

"Mmmm," she hummed, sucking and stroking and licking, making my dick sopping wet with her spit.

I lifted my head to watch her work, her naked ass in the air. Dropping my head, I moaned, "Come sit on my face."

"Hmm?" she replied, her mouth still on me.

"Come sit on my face. I wanna eat your pussy while you suck my dick."

"Maleek, I'm too big. I'll smother you," she protested after letting me slide out of her mouth.

"I don't care."

"Well, I do! I don't want to kill you—oh!"

I sat up and grabbed her, spinning her around until her ass was in my face.

"Damn, I forgot how strong you are. Do you know how much I weigh?" she shrieked.

"Don't care. It doesn't matter. If I die, I'll die happy. Back that ass up and put that pussy on my mouth."

With no further argument, she wriggled her body until I had a nose full of ass and a mouth full of pussy. I went to work, whimpering when I felt her mouth on me again. I devolved into something totally untamed, sucking her whole damn pussy, gripping her soft ass, and not giving a fuck if I ever took the shallowest of breaths again.

Smacking her ass, I garbled, "Ride my face," into her pussy.

"Hmm?" she replied, my dick somewhere in her esophagus as I jiggled her ass cheeks and smacked her butt again. I guessed she got the message because she started bouncing up and down on my mouth, soon grinding on my tongue, my dick forgotten as she whined, "Ohhhhhh, shit!"

I licked and sucked and slurped and nibbled, gripping her ass so tightly that I was sure I'd leave handprints on it when I was done. When her ride became chaotic, her pussy sliding from my chin to my nose, I knew she'd hit her peak, eventually collapsing onto my body and taking her sweet pussy from my mouth.

Licking my lips, I said, "Kiss me so you can taste this pussy, too."

Slowly, she rotated her body until her face hovered over mine, her pussy grazing my dick. I damn near cried at feeling that heat on me, and when our mouths connected, we both filled the room with moans of pleasure. We switched positions with me on top and between her thick thighs, my dick dripping as I sucked one titty while squeezing the other. Nuri's body was like a damn magical theme park, all luscious curves and dips and soft skin. Exploring her frame with its peaks and valleys was akin to taking a cross-country road trip to heaven.

I moved to the opposite breast as she held the back of my head. When she begged, "Put it in," I nodded, was about to dive into that good pussy of hers but said, "Hold on a sec."

"What?" she whined as I stood and walked over to her bedside table, my dick hard and ready. Once I found what I needed in the drawer, I returned to her on the floor, powering the rose on.

"Oh," she breathed, jerking when I placed the toy to her clit.

"Hold it for me, baby," I said, watching as she took possession of the toy.

She released a tortured moan as the rose sucked her bud while I eased inside her. She felt so fucking good that I had to slap the floor to keep from screaming.

"Baby...am I hurting you?" My words came out harsh and strained.

"No. You could never hurt me," she whimpered.

I stilled inside her, my breathing ragged as I murmured, "I missed this pussy so damn much!"

Lifting her head, she kissed me as I eased back and slowly slid forward, the room populated with the buzzing of the rose, our harsh breathing, and the smell of our sex.

Fucking paradise.

I'd shut my eyes and was close to busting when she started twitching, her breathing growing more and more staccato as her walls began to quake around me. I felt liquid gush from her as she grabbed my face and sobbed, "I love you. I love you so much, Maleek!"

She squirted.

She fucking squirted.

Opening my eyes and gazing down at her as my nut tore through me, I grunted, "I...love...you...so...much...more!"

"You squirted," I said into the darkness of our room.

"Is that what that was? Wow. That felt crazy, but I liked it," Nuri replied into my chest. We were in bed, skin to skin and groggy from fucking on our bedroom floor like it was the end of the world.

"So did I."

"Maleek?"

"Yeah, baby?"

"I started taking the pills again."

"Okay," I responded. "You're not ready to try for another baby?"

"No. I think we should wait a while. I...I'm just telling you about the pills, so you won't think tonight was about me trying to get pregnant."

"I didn't think it was, but what *was* tonight about?"

"I needed you. I needed the connection. I missed it."

"Me too. Hey, I can get a vasectomy, so you don't have to take the pill."

"Why? You don't *ever* want kids?"

"I do. I want you to have my baby, but it feels like everything is on you when it shouldn't be. Your body is taking all the hits and I hate it."

"See how safe I am with you?" she whispered, her voice unsteady.

"You'll always be safe with me, baby. *Always.*"

"I don't mind taking the pills. I want to have your child one day."

I kissed the top of her head. "Okay."

"Maleek...I was on Instagram today and I saw this post, a random picture of the principal at Rogers Elementary School. Last year, while I was still working there as a teacher, something happened that I'm still not over. There was a shooting."

"Baby...what?"

"Yeah, it was the ex-husband of one of my coworkers, a fellow teacher. Her classroom was next door to mine. They were in the middle of a rough divorce and a child custody battle. I guess he just snapped. He entered the school and started shooting. Luckily, the resource officer was quickly able to subdue him, and no one was hurt, but...I-I froze. I heard those gunshots coming from down the hall, and I froze. We were trained on what to do. I was supposed to protect those kids and I fucking froze! If they'd died, it would've been on me because I did nothing to keep them safe." She was crying now, and my heart broke for her.

"Nuri, you're not at fault for that. I probably would've frozen, too. Nothing, no amount of training, can prepare a person for some shit like that. You went to school to be a teacher, not a fucking body-guard or Secret Service Agent."

"No, can't you see? That's why I quit my job. I knew I didn't need to be a teacher anymore. I failed my students! I shouldn't be around kids at all. Not Jules, not Junior, and that's why our baby was taken from us. Because of what I did...or actually, what I *didn't* do."

I sat up, turning the bedside lamp on. "Nuri, look at me." When her eyes met mine, I continued, "I want you to hear every word I'm about to say. Losing our baby was beyond our control, beyond *your* control. It's fucked up, it hurts, and if anyone is to blame, it's me. I'm the one with the crazy-ass ex. No, she hasn't done anything in a while, but I know the possibility of her popping up is stressful. I'm the one with two kids to take care of. I'm the one who's gone all the damn time. If anyone caused this, I did."

"No, you didn't," she countered. "I kept so much inside—the shooting, my family. That can't be good for a baby. I—"

By then, we were both crying, and as painful as this conversation was, I knew it was overdue.

I shook my head. "No. How about this? I won't blame myself if you don't blame yourself, and both our asses start seeing a therapist. I don't want us to get lost in this shit and ruin what we have. I don't want to lose *you*. I won't survive that."

She nodded, reaching up and pulling my face down to hers. "Okay," she agreed before giving me the sweetest, softest kiss. "Deal."

"Thank you," I murmured before sliding down her body and burying my face between her legs...again.

36

NURI

I was so nervous that my hands shook as I stood there. It was mid March, and the regular season was ending in a month or so. Maleek had signed the required waiver, and Junior's dream was finally coming true. He was riding the Zamboni. The smile he wore as he was being strapped into the swivel seat was definitely priceless, and while I was happy that *he* was happy, I'd made the mistake of watching some videos about this machine and ran across a few where more than one caught fire. I damn near had a nervous breakdown when I saw those. It took some serious reassurance from Maleek for me to go along with it, but here I was, standing front and center filming Junior having the time of his young life. He grinned and waved as the driver navigated their path on the ice. The Zamboni's main function was to resurface the relatively thin layer of ice that comprised the game space, but it was on nearly every fan's bucket list to hitch a ride on one at least once in their lifetime. For others, they dreamt of actually driving one. As for me, I just wanted this to be over and for Junior to be safe and sound on ice-less ground.

It was cute, though, the way he was eating up the enthusiasm the crowd generously gave him, almost as cute as he was in his jacket, his curly hair peeking from underneath his Sires skull cap.

When he finally climbed down from the machine, he flew to me, smiling brightly as he said, "That was lit!"

Hugging him, I said, "I bet it was!"

Maleek was moving fast, advancing the puck into the offensive zone toward their opponent's goal, but he couldn't make a shot because of a guy from the other team who was on him. The guy was too close to Maleek, blocking his access to the goal. Then, Maleek somehow got the puck past him to Ford on his left. Ford quickly slapped the puck toward the goal, but unfortunately, the opponent's goalie blocked it, eliciting a loud chorus of moans and more than a few obscenities from Sires fans, including me and Miss Iesha. Oh, and Coco, too.

The game continued on with its usual brutality and intensity. Maleek was propelled into the glass near us at one point. I hated seeing him get shoved and hit as much as I hated seeing the resulting bruises on his body afterwards, but he loved this game. He wouldn't be happy without it.

As he pushed off the glass, he skated the couple feet to where we sat, slapping it and pointing at me, a big grin on his face. I returned his smile, thinking just how much I loved me some Maleek Jones.

MALEEK

I was heading back to the locker room after doing press. I'd decided I wanted Jules and/or Junior in there with me after the next home game. A lot of the guys had their kids with them when they answered the reporters' questions. It was only right that I did the same with my siblings.

I was worn out but happy we'd managed to get a win tonight, happy and ready to go home and climb into bed with my wife. I was sitting on the bench trying to figure out how I could summon enough energy to at least eat her pussy or maybe her ass when Ford dropped a hand on my shoulder.

"Good game, Jones! Or as Stick would say, *Hotline Bling!*" Ford said.

I looked up at him and laughed. "Stick is stupid, but he is one hell of a goalie."

"Facts. Hey, you seen that video Tasha posted? I just ran across it on IG."

I frowned. "I just left press. I ain't had time to check social media. What she saying in it?" I really didn't care as long as she kept her mouth off Nuri. She could say whatever she wanted about me.

"She...uh, you just gotta see it."

Ford had just finished that statement when my phone buzzed. I pulled it out of my duffel and saw that Rapp had texted me a link, the link to Tasha's video, to be exact. I didn't even know where the hell Rapp was at that moment.

I scratched my forehead before tapping on the link. After watching the video twice, I stood, mumbling, "Later," to Ford before leaving the locker room and the arena.

"Y'all see this bitch? This is the ho' my man of seven fucking years left me for! Look at her! She ain't nowhere near my league! But I guess he likes 'em basic. Look at those braids. Ew!" Tasha said, providing commentary on a cell phone video of Nuri recording and cheering Junior on as he rode the Zamboni. Apparently, the footage was recorded by Tasha. This was my fourth time watching the video, and my reaction was the same every time—rage.

"I sacrificed my best years for Maleek Jones, and he left me to wife a damn water buffalo! Look at her ass! He has a whole gym in his house, and I bet her fat ass doesn't even know where it is! My fellow women, let this be a cautionary tale for you. Don't waste your time keeping your hair and nails done and your body tight for a simple-ass Memphis nigga 'cause all he gon' do is leave you for a bitch with raggedy braids and cellulite!" Tasha continued.

Taking a deep breath, I tapped out of Instagram and went to my text messages, replying to Nuri's *Where are you?* message with, *I'll be home in a few minutes.* Then I slid my phone into the pocket of my sweatpants and climbed out my Jeep, making my way to the front door. I rang the doorbell, waited a whole second, and rang it again.

When it swung open to reveal Tasha in short shorts and a t-shirt, my eyes narrowed.

"Maleek? The hell are you doing here?" she snapped.

I licked my lips as I shoved my hands into the kangaroo pocket of my hoodie. "I need to talk to you. Can I come in?"

"I'm busy right now," she said.

"What? You on IG Live or something? You tryna be an influencer now?"

"I've *been* an influencer, baby, and yes, I *am* on IG Live. I'm giving relationship advice."

"Okay..."

"You wanna be on my live or something?"

"Tash, I don't give a fuck about that. I just need to talk to you."

She stared at me before smiling widely. "You saw my video, the one of your...wife. Did it make you come to your senses."

I returned her smile. "Something like that."

"Come on in, then."

I followed her through the familiar foyer of her mother's house into the huge formal living room, where she had a ring light set up. Her cell phone was in a holder in the center of the ring. She was really taking this influencer shit seriously. Good for her.

Plopping down on the sofa, her phone facing her, she announced, "I'm back, guys! Guess who was at the door!" She paused, mouthing something. I figured out she was reading comments when she said, "You got it, @yourfavesfave! It's my ex. Y'all wanna see him beg?"

I fought not to roll my eyes, staying glued to my spot beyond the light.

Looking up at me, she said, "My people wanna see you." She patted the sofa cushion beside her. "Come have a seat."

I did, ignoring the phone and her audience as she returned her attention to them.

She was animated as she spoke. "Guys, this is Maleek...Yes, he *is* fine, @Younggiftedwon. Okay, Maleek, what is it you need to say to me?"

She was looking at me now. Good, because I needed her undivided attention.

"I saw the video, and I want to ask you a favor," I began. "I want you to leave my wife out of your shit. She didn't do anything to you. She was never in a relationship with you. *I* was. You're gonna believe what you wanna believe, but I did not cheat on you with her. I didn't leave you. *You* left *me*. I know I hurt you by not trying to fix us, but I told you my heart hadn't been in our relationship in a long time, probably years, if I'm being honest. I'm sorry about that. You deserved better. You were good to me, and I appreciate that you were committed to me. I really do. I was fucked up. I can admit that. So, you can post whatever you want about me, call me names, make fun of me. The truth about me is bad enough, but feel free to lie, whatever you need to do to purge me from your heart. Seriously, *whatever* you need to do. I can take it. I deserve it, but you gotta stop fucking with my wife."

She looked shocked but quickly schooled her expression. "So, you came over here to beg on that bitch's behalf—"

"Nope. She ain't nobody's bitch. She's my *wife*. Nothing you post or say is gonna change that. I'm trying to appeal to you rather than file harassment charges, but this is the last time I'm bypassing the police. Stop this shit. NOW. Damn, you've got more fucking self-respect than this. I *know* you do. Let it go, Tash."

Her mouth was hanging open when I stood from the sofa and left.

NURI

"You're up," he said, his voice low, smooth, and panty-dropping. You know, the usual.

I nodded, holding up my cell as I sat on his side of the bed. "I am. Been perusing IG. Ran across some interesting stuff, too."

In the low lamp light, he set his trusty duffel bag in one of the accent chairs sitting a few feet from the bed. He walked over to me, sliding his hands in the front pocket of his hoodie, his head tilted to the side, his eyes on me. Damn, he was fine.

"You saw Tasha's live?" he asked. "She left it up?"

"She removed it, but someone recorded it. It's been shared multiple times. So yeah...I saw it."

He pulled his hands from the pocket, crossing his arms over his chest. "And you're not mad about me going to see her," he observed.

"I'm not. The only reason I'm still up is because I've been trying to figure something out."

"What's that, baby?"

"Exactly how much pussy do you want?"

He was smiling now, his brow furrowed in contrast. "What?"

"How much pussy do you want? Also, would you like for me to suck your dick from the back? I can watch some porn for instructions. I'll do just about anything except anal. Still *hell no* to that."

I watched as he laughed, his eyes crinkling at the corners, Adam's apple bouncing, one big hand splayed on his chest as his head fell back. Once he finally regained his composure, he said, "Yo, you're crazy!" Sitting beside me on the bed, he grasped my hand. "But I love your crazy ass. Listen, I couldn't let that shit Tasha did slide. I'm not sure if it was a good idea to confront her or if she really heard me, but I knew I had to do something."

Leaning in close to his face, I gently pecked his plush lips and smiled. "Thank you for defending me, but I could've handled her. I'm itching to curse her out."

"Oh, I know. I've seen you match energy, but I'm your husband, your covering. I'm supposed to defend and protect you. It's my job."

"Hmmm, well...they are tearing her up in the comments, so there's that."

"Good."

We shared another kiss, this one deep and stirring, a preamble to him showing me exactly how much pussy he wanted.

37

MALEEK

"Congratulations on a great season. I'm looking forward to seeing you guys capture the Stanley Cup next year," he said. I knew this man was one of my team's owners. I also knew he'd be at this end-of-season celebration. Still, I was star-struck like a motherfucker. So was Nuri.

"Uh...thank you, sir. It's...can I get your autograph?" I babbled.

Big South smiled. "Yeah. No problem."

Then we stood there, him looking at me and me looking at him until my damn brain stopped sputtering. "Oh! Baby, you got a pen and paper?" I asked my wife, turning to see her big doe eyes glued to this legend. I couldn't even be mad about it.

"Nuri?" I tried again.

"Huh?" She blinked a few times before adding, "Oh! You were talking to me! Yes, let me see." After digging in her purse, she pulled out a pink ink pen and a baby blue sticky note pad. Shit, whatever.

Nuri and I watched him sign his name like we were front row at one of his concerts before he retired. He handed the pad back to Nuri, and I had to stop myself from snatching it out of her hand.

I swear her eyes were glowing as she looked down at the illegible writing and said, "Woooow, it's beautiful."

"Thanks," he replied. "Good chatting with y'all. I'ma see if I can meet some more of your teammates, Maleek." And then he was gone.

"Damn, he's big," Nuri said, staring after him.

"What you mean, *he's big?* I ain't exactly little," I countered. Yeah, I was Stanning him, too, but I had recovered a little.

"You're not. I'm just saying...did you see him?"

"Yeah, I saw him. Shit."

"Oh! Is that Bianca Bambina?" Nuri shrieked. "She's gorgeous!"

I followed her line of sight to see that it *was* her. Bianca Bambina was hands down one of the best lady MCs in the business and also one of the Sires' co-owners. I didn't know *she'd* be here. Like, wow!

"Yep, that's her. I wonder if Rapp knows she's here. He's a Bianca B fanatic for real," I mused.

Nuri smirked. "So, Rapp is a BB Baby? He be putting baby emojis in her IG comments?"

"Shiiiit, probably."

We laughed but stopped when we saw Rapp's grown ass scream Bianca's name and take off running toward her.

"Wow," I muttered.

"Double wow," Nuri agreed.

"Was that Rapp?" That was Ford, who'd popped up out of thin air.

"Unfortunately, yes," I confirmed.

"Goofy ass," Ford muttered. Then he turned to Nuri, grinning at her. "Hey, Mrs. Jooooones."

"Motherfucker, don't speak to my wife," I growled.

"Maleek!" Nuri screeched.

"Got dayum! I was just being hospitable. Let me go mess with Stick and Coco, since you wanna be petty. Bye. Mrs. Jooooones." He started walking away, and before I could threaten him, Jules and

Junior ran into me. Like, they literally slammed full speed into my body.

"Whoa! Where's Mama Iesha? Y'all lost her?" I quipped.

"She's coming!" Jules chirped. Every time she opened her mouth to speak, my heart swelled a little bit more. I followed the finger she was pointing and found my mother rushing toward us.

"Sorry, they saw you and couldn't wait to tell you about the little trucks they got to drive on the ice over in the arena."

"They weren't trucks, Mama Iesha! They were mini-Zambonis!" Junior corrected her.

"Oh, yeah. I better get that right," Ma replied with a wink. The party was being held in one of the buildings adjacent to our home arena, a part of the Sires complex. There was music and food and—

"Big South! Is that Big South?!" my mom trilled.

"It is! Wanna meet him?" Nuri offered.

"Yes!" my mom chimed.

"Come on, kids," I said. "We're going, too." It wasn't that I was insecure. I knew my wife loved me, but shit, this nigga was Big South. I didn't know a heterosexual woman alive who didn't want him.

"I ain't have no idea this many negroes could ice skate! When my nephew invited me to come to this here shindig, I was like, you going to see some negroes who ice skate? Count me in!" This man, Big South's uncle, was funny as hell. Word was, he was also my agent's father-in-law. I was going to have to confirm this shit with Nate, because wow! Nate's wife had a whole PhD, and *this* was her father? Maybe she was adopted...

"Yeah, it's a bunch of us who can ice skate, but that's not all we do on the team," I explained. "It's all about making goals."

"That's right. But what I wanna know is how y'all kick the ball with them skates on," he said, taking a bite out of a rib. "Whoever cooked this must ain't have no good barrel grill. That's the only way to cook ribs. Hey, y'all play with sticks, don't you? Y'all hit the football with the stick? Awww, shit! Gotta call."

I kid you not, this man wiped his hands on a napkin and tapped the button on a Bluetooth earpiece. Yes, he was actually wearing a Bluetooth earpiece.

"What-up-there-now?! Huh? What? Speak up, shit! Uh-huh...uh-huh...turn it off, slap the side of it, and turn it back on. Yeah...okay...goodbye." He ended the call and went back in on his ribs. "That was my wife. Her car acting up."

Her car?

The fuck?

Nuri returned to the table with a second plate for me and a bottled water for herself.

"Thank you, baby," I said, kissing her cheek after she reclaimed her seat beside me. "Baby, this is Mr. Lee Chester, Big South's uncle. Mr. Lee, this is my wife, Nuri Jones."

"Nice to meet you, Mr. Lee. I love your nephew's music," Nuri gushed.

"Mmhmm, you can call me Unc. Everybody calls me Unc. Shole is pretty." His eyes still on Nuri, he added, "Mystique, you like 'em thick like I like 'em! She a brick house! Hahaaaa!"

First of all, Mystique?

Second of all, this couldn't really be Big South's uncle...could it?

"Uh, thank you...I think," I said.

"Welcome. She reminds me of my Kimmy 'bout the body, but my Kimmy dark. I like 'em dark, too. Shit, they got any beer? Let me go see. I'm thirsty as a cat with two tails and a hammer toe!" He left the table and Nuri and I stared at each other for a second before we both fell out laughing.

"Your mom looks so cute over there talking to your coach," Nuri observed a few minutes later.

"Where? What coach?" I asked before spotting them. Darryl Lampkin, our head coach, was all in my mother's face grinning and shit. The kids were at the table with them, but still...

"He better not get too damn close," I mumbled.

"You're tripping. I think they look adorable," Nuri reiterated.

"My mama ain't supposed to look cute or adorable with no nigga up in her face."

"Woooooow," Nuri said, rolling her eyes.

Changing the subject before I did something that would get me fired, I asked, "You having a good time?"

She nodded. "Yeah, being a Sires WAG is lit!"

I chuckled. "Well, being your husband is lit, too."

"Is it?"

"Hell yeah," I said, leaning in to kiss her neck. "The littest."

"Well, that explains it."

"That explains what?"

"How I ended up pregnant again."

I froze, my lips inches from her neck. "You're what?" We'd only decided to try for another baby like a month earlier.

"I'm pregnant. Again. I know you promised to start my ice skating lessons today, but—"

Lifting my head, I stared into her eyes. "Fuck ice skating. Baby, this is the *best* news!"

She rested a hand on my cheek before softly kissing my lips. "Isn't it?"

EPILOGUE

MALEEK

Dear Son,

 I'm not sure if you'll ever read this letter because I'm not sure I'll ever find the courage to send it to you. First, I want to tell you how proud I am of you. I am extremely proud of the man you've become. I'm proud of your achievements and I am amazed by your talent.

 I want you to know that I deeply regret not being in your life. I could say that I'm sorry, but I know that wouldn't be enough. It wouldn't erase the pain I caused you. The look you wore on your face all those years ago when I told you I was sending you back to Memphis still haunts me. At the time, I thought things would be better that way. Now I know I was wrong. I wish I could have been a stronger, better man, but I wasn't. I'm still not and I still don't know how to be a father, but I know I've created greatness. I've taught your siblings, a brother and a sister, all about you, and they're just as proud of you as I am. I hope you get to meet them someday.

 I love you. I hope you believe that, and I hope that one day you'll forgive me.

 Your father,

Adam Jones, Sr.

I folded the letter, sliding it in the hip pocket of my jeans and blowing out a breath. I'd been in possession of it since I met my siblings. Tucked in the back of the folder of documents I was handed that day in Arkansas was this letter addressed to me from my father. I'd ignored it, acted like it didn't exist until the day my son was born. That day, I decided I needed to know what he had to say. Surely, there was something in that letter that would explain why he didn't feel the same about me as I felt about my namesake the second I laid eyes on him. I would give my life for my boy. Why wasn't my father willing to do the same?

I still didn't understand it, but at least I could talk about it instead of letting my feelings pile up inside me and affect my marriage, my family. As I sat in the office lobby of Mr. Alvin Charles, my therapist, I felt like thanking Nathan Moore for the millionth time. He'd recommended him to me, said he was a miracle worker. I wasn't sure if he was all that, but he was good. Nuri was in the same building talking to her own therapist. I was smiling at the thought of her when my name was called. Lifting from my chair, I continued smiling as I made my way into the inner office.

———

I still loved hockey, and although it would always be my first love in a lot of ways, it'd moved down the list from being my *main* love. Now it fell somewhere below my family—my wife, my mom, my sister, my brother, and my baby.

My son.

I loved Little Maleek more than I knew I could love anyone. Holding him was my favorite pastime, and now that he was three months old and chunky as hell, I wasn't scared of breaking him anymore. Now, I was damn near constantly kissing his chubby cheeks and sniffing his neck. Don't judge me, judge your mama. I loved how he looked up at me with his mother's round eyes, his skin tone mirroring mine. He was a perfect combination of us.

"Y'all look so cute," Nuri said, climbing in bed beside us.

"We know," I responded.

She rolled her eyes.

"You feeling okay?" I asked, reaching over to lay my hand on her stomach. She wasn't showing yet, but we had another one on the way.

"This baby is still kicking my ass, but I'm managing. I guess every pregnancy is going to be like this. The reward is worth it, though."

"Yeah. Hey, have I told you how much I love you today, Mrs. Jones?"

Grinning, she leaned in to kiss me. "I think you just did, and I love you, too, Mr. Jones."

"Ewwwwww!" Junior yelled as he and Jules burst in our bedroom and climbed into bed with us. "Y'all *always* kissing!"

Grabbing the remote control from the bedside table, Nuri said, "That's what married people do, Junior."

"Then I'm *never* getting married!" Junior declared.

I chuckled before asking, "What movie we watching tonight, guys?"

"*Encanto!*" Jules sang as she held Little Maleek's hand and smiled at him.

"Oh, god, please no!" Junior groaned.

ABOUT THE AUTHOR

A true southern girl, Alexandria House has an affinity for a good banana pudding, Neo Soul music, and tall black men in suits. When this music-loving fashionista is not shopping, she's writing steamy stories about real black love.

ALSO BY ALEXANDRIA HOUSE

The Love After Series

Higher Love

Made to Love

Real Love

The Strickland Sisters Series

Stay with Me

Believe in Me

Be with Me

The McClain Brothers Series

Let Me Love You

Let Me Hold You

Let Me Show You

Let Me Free You

Let Me Please You (A McClain Family Novella)

The Them Boys Series

Set

Jah

Shu

The Romey U Series

Teach Me

Touch Me

Temper Me

The St. Louis Cyclones Series

Flagrant

Technical

Personal

The St. Louis Sires Series

Goal

Short Works

Baby, Be Mine

Merry Christmas, Baby

Always My Baby

Should've Been

All I Want

New Year, New Boo?

Sanctuary (Paranormal)

the exhibition

Jingle Mingle

Joonteenth

F*cking on the 4th

Schoolhouse THOT

Short Story Collections

the love deluxe mixtape

the love galore mixtape

the love infinite mixtape

The Holiday Shorts

Poetry

The Book of Nyles

Text alexhouse to (833) 445-0326 to be notified of new releases!

Printed in Great Britain
by Amazon

38177285R00119